No
Fairy Tales

Written By: Miaya Deneen Bridgett

Edited By: Kendall Aguilera

Cover By: Gabriel Velez

It took a long time, but we're here, or at least I'm here waiting for him to show up. I should have known that I was in trouble, or better yet, that the road ahead would be long. Was this road worth it? I've crushed a lot of people to get here. But I am here, and I am happy. Isn't that what life is: a long struggle to find happiness? So why am I so nervous? I guess it started with him. After all, he's propelled every major decision I have ever made in my life- him and my pride.

Yet, I still can't believe that fifteen years has already passed. It hardly seems fathomable. Nevertheless, I'm here. I'm alive- living in this moment. It's been blood, sweat, and tears. It has been fifteen years, and I can finally see him in the flesh and tell him how I felt and how I still feel. I've known him since forever. He's still a nerd. I am still most likely the most interesting person that he knows.

So why am I so fucking nervous? I can't believe this shit! Me? Nervous?

When I first saw him, I remember that I did not love him right away. How could I? He was a dorky, skinny, white guy, who never spoke much- extremely introverted. I, on the other hand, was extroverted and had all of the shape of a young Cleopatra. I was the one passing him by like a Pharcyde song without giving him a thought. Besides, he wasn't my type. God, sometimes I wish I was that girl now -the standoffish girl looking at him to see to the other side of the room. It sure would have saved me a lot of heartache. It would have saved my husbands' heartache too. But alas, I wasn't that girl anymore.

But I did hold onto myself long enough to let him know that I was 'da bomb'. And he pursued me. Why did he pursue me? I asked myself then and I still ask myself now. Maybe it was because my African-American heritage

3

made me exotic, someone different. Though I highly doubt that. The only thing black about me was my hair and ass.

He represented white America, and yet he was three shades darker than me. But hey, black is black. Maybe he was curious. Maybe he wanted some chocolate-vanilla swirl. Hell, it could have been that. My daddy told me that seventeen year old boys –emphasis on boys- only wanted one thing. Yet, it couldn't have been that. Was it? He did look at me longingly.

He carried my books around school, listened to my girl talk, followed me around like a love-struck puppy, and yet I wasn't fazed at all. One day, he came to my house when I had finally agreed to go out with him. I wasn't there of course. I was at an orchestra recital- representing my school- where our colors, orange and blue, bled from my violin onto the notes and into the ears of the attentive judges. Full of confidence and pride, with a trophy in my

4

school's pocket, I rode the bus home to find my mother

sitting on the steps.

"Who was that boy?" she asked in her deep, husky

tone of voice as she took a long drag off her cigarette. Her

thin fingers enveloped the Virginia Slim so delicately as if

she belonged on the Virginia Slim's billboard. Her other

hand gripped her Miller Genuine Draft. She looked at me

as if she meant business and said again, "Who's dat boy?"

"What boy?" I asked, totally clueless.

"That boy- the white one- he came to our house,

walked up the steps, and told me he was here to pick you

up. Just like that, said 'I'm the guy to pick her up.'" Her

stare was stone-cold and long. She looked curious and

annoyed at the same time. My sweaty palms tightly

grabbed my instrument as her eyes traced mine.

I was bewildered. *Could this fool actually have*

gone up and told my mother that he was the guy coming to

5

pick me up? I thought. No. Not that straggly guy. This would mean he had some …something. *Nah, he doesn't have that kind of something….does he? Oh No. What if she scared him?*

"Well, what did you say?" I asked very nonchalantly.

"I said: 'No, the fuck you aren't,'" my mother barked.

"Mom!" I cried. "Please tell me that you did not say that. I will be so embarrassed if you said that. Oh my God!"

"Well, tell that boy the next time he comes over here. He better be more respectful! I'm the lady of this damn house. Who da fuck does he think he is?"

"Yes, momma!" I said dutifully. I knew my place. No, you did not want to take my momma on, especially when she was on the porch taking long drags off her cigarette and staring into the abyss that is the Westside of Chicago.

However, I did take notice then. Just a little bit. He stood up to my momma, which was very suave even at seventeen. I could visualize him telling my mother that he was going to pick me up. After fifteen years, I still find myself asking if he knew what he was "picking up" that day when he tried to pick me up. I sure as hell didn't. Maybe, if we both knew at the time, we would have run the other way, screaming and kicking in the opposite direction.

I didn't know that my heart was going to be picked up and dropped off by him a million and one times since that day. Yet, like castaway that washed up on shore, I am here today- a little torn and worn. Some say unscathed and blessed. All I know is that I wouldn't take our love back, scars and all.

2

I took notice after he plundered my family's fort, and something in me had changed. He was not that straggly haired kid with acne for days. He showed me that he had gumption. He took on my mother and was not afraid of her. My mother's stare could bring a whole army down. But he stood up to her. It was then that I started feeling for him- just a little bit.

He finally cornered me at school and grabbed my books. "Why did you flake out?" He looked at me questioningly. His eyes were locked onto mine. I could feel him staring deep into my soul for an answer. He had my full attention.

"I didn't flake out," I lied. I knew I flaked out, or at least, I knew I forgot. I didn't take him seriously. He told me that he was going to pick me up, but I had dismissed him.

"Yes, you did." He wasn't letting up. He was tenacious at seventeen! This was a new kind of guy- a guy I could respect. He wasn't afraid to challenge me.

"Look, I forgot that we were supposed to chill. I mean, I had a recital. You know it's important to me. I play first chair."

Yes, I found my confidence during his third degree. Where did I drop it off?

"For real? I didn't know you were first at anything," he teased.

"Well, I am for your information. Look we can chill and all, but my momma said you were mad disrespectful to her." I looked at him inquisitively. I wanted to ask him more, but I didn't. I was caught in his intensity, his confidence, his charm.

"Mad dis-re-spec-?" he said laughing at me.

I can't believe this fool is laughing at me, I thought.

9

"Hells yeah. You were mad disrespectful to my momma. She said you told her that you were 'the guy coming to pick me up.'" I looked at him curiously.

"Yes, I did," he said so sure of himself.

How the hell is he so sure of himself all of sudden?

"Hmmm. Well, don't do that shit again, but you can pick me up and take me to the movies." I snapped and flirted a little. After all, he did stand up to my momma.

"Okay, how about this weekend?" He shrugged.

He just doesn't quit, does he?

"Sure. Now can I have my books back?" I teased. "I'm going to be late for class."

"Yup, I'm done with you anyway." He handed my books back. I turned around so he couldn't see me blush. I didn't want to admit defeat by showing him that I was interested... because I was. It was the first time that I really took notice of him. It was also the first time that he

10

made my heart skip a little. We walked away, and I had no idea what I was getting into. I only knew that I really didn't want him to leave. If my future self could have come through a warp hole, grabbed me, and tell me –no, not him. Yup, that would have been the perfect time to do it....I think.

3

He picked me up on time. It was really early- field trip early- in an old pick-up truck. Half of the bumper was off. It looked old, run down, and barely looked legal. He told me it was his dad's work truck, and that he had to return it- well, we had to return it.

"Get in," he said with a wide smirk, almost full grin. His hair fell below his eyebrow. He swept it back. I felt as if I wanted to pull his hair back for him.

What is this feeling? I don't know what it is, but it's getting warm in here. "So what movie are we going to

11

see?" I asked trying to hold back my anxiety. My palms were dripping with sweat.

Why am I nervous? This is just crazy. It's only skinny, nerdy Tony from math class. We had two classes together, and I never noticed him then. So chill the hell out already!

"We're not," he said with his smirk appearing wider.

It almost looks like a full-fledged grin.

"What. No movie? You told me… "

"I told you we might go see a movie, but I have something better in mind. I just need to return my dad's truck. Then we will hop on the train and get to where we will be."

"Which is?" I pressed.

"A surprise." *Yup, full-fledged grin. What is he up to?*

"Look, I read Stephen King. You aren't going to cut me into little pieces are you? Just know that my mom will hunt you down and kill you."

"Oh my god! Would you just quit it? It's out of your control. It's a surprise. Chill the hell out. No one is going to 'cut you up into pieces.' Jesus, where do you get this stuff from?"

"I told you that I read Stephen King," I snapped back. "You know, you may be a little more trouble than you're worth."

Jesus, I knew back then he would be trouble. Yet, I welcomed it. I welcomed this "trouble" into my life. Holy snikees, Batman, I welcomed Tony into my life. But I only noticed Tony then. I didn't really welcome Tony until we arrived at his surprise.

4

After we dropped his dad's car off, we got onto the "El train". We headed into down-town, Chicago. I looked out the window because I had never seen this part of the city before. The whole time I looked out the window, his eyes were on me- tracing me- remembering my every curve. I didn't see him do this, but I knew he was watching me. I was the mysterious, quirky girl that captivated him. I was an intricate mechanical device. He just wanted to see how I worked. He wanted to break me apart and put me back together.

Sometimes, I wonder if he knew that once he opened me- tinkered with this and that, would he understand the permanent changes that he would be making to my design. I don't think he cared. For now, he just watched me while I gazed outside.

I looked at the houses and trees and cars and vacant lots. I looked at the city and thought to myself that it was so beautiful- so ugly beautiful. I thought how I would not have seen this had he not showed me. My identity was developing, and he was the one mapping it. I took a little more notice of him.

We got off the train, and like a little cub following the momma bear, I followed him passed the street lights, passed the homeless people loitering on the sidewalks, passed the skyscrapers. For blocks and blocks, I followed him dutifully. He was taking me to *his* spot, and so I began to relax.

We arrived at a park next to a pier. People were all about- barbequing and enjoying life. I didn't think anyone could enjoy this city. I lived in the ghetto, and other than running into your house when shots were fired, there wasn't too much barbequing going on, except in the

15

summer. And this was the beginning of fall. People were living their lives. It gave me an inner peace that wasn't in my life before. *He* gave it to me- this peace.

But that wasn't the surprise. He took me by the hand. He made me walk up to what appeared to be a lake. Then, he led me down a small stairway.

"Is this it? I mean, where are we going? This shit is making me nervous." I did feel nervous. This was a new experience, and I had no idea where he was taking me. Yet, at the same time, I felt safe. I felt warm. I felt happy.

"Oh my god. Chill out. I'm taking you to a special place," he teased.

Oh my God, Jade. Don't overdo it. Don't scare him away by your incessant worrying.

"Is this where you take all of the girls?" I teased.

"No, just the cute ones," he teased back.

"I better be the only one," I snapped.

16

I followed him down some more concrete stairs. They got tinier as we walked down them. God, the city didn't fix anything back then. I thought for sure I was going to fall into the lake. That would have been so bogus. Then we climbed up some stairs that defied even more logic because they got tinier too. It was as if our physical environment was changing with each step. We both trudged on, and I looked out onto the water. It was beautiful- simply breathtaking.

We walked up to this gorgeous beach-like area. It was manmade- probably made for all of the rich people who could live on this side of town. We walked through the soft sand. He turned towards the waves. I watched him, and followed. He playfully kicked up some water towards me. I got wet, the water hit my hair, and then I got mad.

I wanted payback. I ran up to him and kicked some water into his direction. Laughing, he met my challenge, and this battle continued for the next ten minutes. I noticed him. I noticed that he never accepted defeat. He kind of mirrored me in that aspect. I felt that he was something more than a seventeen year old boy- almost a kindred spirit.

We walked up another set of stairs adjacent to the pier and then sat down. We were panting. I can't believe we expended expelled so much energy playing in the water. But now we were calmly sitting on the pier, shoulder to shoulder. I could see yachts on the lake off the horizon. I saw the sun shimmer on the water. The water looked like diamonds. I looked around, and quickly realized we were the only ones there.

It felt like an eternity. Silence surrounded me, and I felt like I was suspended in time. The water crashing along the pier was hypnotizing me. I felt as if I was having an out-of-body experience because I had never been so calm and at peace. I was in the shade, but my spirit was in the sun dancing on the water. Then the most fateful thing happened. He broke the silence.

"Whadya say, Jade? Whadya say?" He asked.

He awakened me from my hypnotic state. My gaze went from the blue diamonds of the water to his eyes. His eyes were blue, but they shined like diamonds as well. All of a sudden, I didn't just notice him. I imploded. His eyes didn't reflect the water, but the depths of my soul. He imprinted on my heart.

All of a sudden he wasn't just a guy. He was the captor of my heart. He was the reason that spring made flowers. He was the reason that I was placed on this green earth. Here, awakening me, was my... my soul mate. Somehow I already knew he was my everything. He

19

transformed into something much more than a seventeen year old boy. He became Tony, Guardian and Keeper of Jade's heart.

Did he feel it too? I'll never know.

I laugh at it now in my older years. I'm stunned at how a seventeen year old could become the guardian of my heart. Nevertheless, he held the key to my intricate lock. "Hmph! He always had the key. I guess that means I am flawlessly fated. Oh well."

Nevertheless, I imploded. We sat for a while, and I was in awe how in less than a week, a straggly haired, skinny guy could transform himself into Brad Pitt, or something like him... but it happened. We sat and watched the sun dance on diamonds. When it was time for us to go, I didn't want to leave this magical place. I wanted to suspend time and live in this moment forever. I guess good things always come to an end. Why should this be any different? *Why? Because I love him. I love him more than myself for some reason starting that day.*

We left the pier and the sun and the diamonds. We walked away side by side- together, and I found myself turning my head back. I wanted to see if I could recapture the magic, and steal one last moment. Yet, the downside of magic's wonder and splendor is the sonic speed in which it fleets. It shows its face, runs and hides, and becomes a unicorn or a leprechaun, something enchanted and yet impossible. It becomes the things that men, including him, would later forget.

He took me home that evening. As I watched the sun going down on the horizon, I sat on the train that showed me pictures of the same city but in reverse. I was forever changed. In my soul, a hole was filled. In his hand, was my heart. I was seventeen, but I wasn't stupid. Something happened to me that I could never take back.

Even if I wanted to take it back, which I did over the years, I couldn't. I just couldn't.

5

I couldn't wait to see Tony at school the next day. I couldn't wait to see his hair fall below his eyes and shadow his face. I couldn't wait to see him outside of my class-waiting to hold my books. I was really giddy. I was really happy. I was really in love.

Whatever side effect of love existed, I had it. I couldn't get him out of my mind. My heart was racing faster than any exercise I went through in gym class. Even Mrs. Vega, my orchestra instructor, could not erase the happiness that I felt in my heart with her incessant criticism.

"Jade," she shrieked.

"Yes, Mrs. Vega?" I was dreading the embarrassment from being called out. I typically wasn't embarrassed for being called out. Mrs. Vega almost always called me out. Her iconic shrill voice brought fear to all of her students. She looked like Carmen from the Opera comique. She had long black curly hair, beautiful dark brown eyes, and olive skin. She reminded me of a goddess from Greek mythology. But the way she screamed at you when your pitch was too high or too low could raise the dead. Yet, I wasn't embarrassed.

This time, however, I was embarrassed because I thought love was written all over my face. My face was crimson red, and I swear that I had a neon sign on it that read "I love Tony!" I was mortified and very paranoid. My love was branded on my heart, and I thought it might as well be branded on my forehead, too.

"Jade, you are making a lot of mistakes! Where is your head today? It's staccato. It's playful. It's forte. Why are you playing long notes? Why are you playing slow? You're also playing soft- basically the reverse of what you're supposed to be playing! So where is your head, love?"

"I'm sorry, Mrs. Vega. It won't happen again." I picked up my violin in dread and defeat. *Damn it, is it that obvious? It is branded on my forehead, and now Mrs. Vega knows. At this rate, everyone will be teasing me by lunch.*

"No worries, love. I want to see you after class though," she said. "Okay, everyone! Let's take it from the top."

The class murmured, whispered, and I knew it was about me. The first chair messed up. I guess they thought that the mighty had finally fallen. Maybe they just took advantage of the extra time to talk and laugh at their own lives. Half of me was embarrassed, but the other half

couldn't give a shit. I was in love, and it was the happiest

feeling in my life.

The time dragged on the other half of the period. I

was feeling like I was losing out on invaluable time- the

time that Tony and I would share as he escorted me to

class. My palms began to sweat as I thought of him. My

bow kept slipping out of my hand. Quickly, I pulled my

head out of my ass and got my act together. *I'm first chair.*

I can't screw up now. Mrs. Perfection. Mrs. Perfect! The

bell rang, and my heart lifted and raced as if I were running

for Olympic Gold. Yet, out of nowhere, came a shrill and

familiar voice that stopped me dead in my tracks.

"Jade?"

"Yes, Mrs. Vega?" *Damn it. I fucking forgot. If I'm*

not there, Tony won't see me. Oh my God. What if he

thinks I don't like him? Ugh! I was drenched in panic, but it wasn't as harsh as being found out- being found out that I was in love. I had a reputation to protect: First chair who is serious about her shit! I learned to play only four years ago and somehow became extremely good, extremely fast. I was supposed to lift my family out of poverty, go out, and be somebody.

To be somebody, I needed discipline. I needed clarity and focus. I needed scholarships to good colleges. I needed to play for the Chicago Symphony Orchestra. What I did not need was a distraction. What I did not need was a boy with dirty blonde or brown or whatever you call it hair. What I needed, like one needed the plague, was blue eyes that shimmered like diamonds. Tony was the plague on my heart. He was contagious and infectious, and Mrs. Vega was the doctor giving me the diagnosis.

"Jade is everything okay? You seemed distracted."

Shit, the jig is up.

"I'm good. I've just been a little overwhelmed lately." *Technically, that was true. I mean, I am overwhelmed by this boy who in less than a week went from my gopher to my spiritual gatekeeper. I guess that is overwhelming for anyone, especially a seventeen year old girl.*

"Okay, good... because you know our concerts are coming up and there will be recruiters in the audience watching you. I need you to have your best game face on. This is for the whole iota. You cannot afford to watch what you've been working for go down the drain. Just relax, and be happy okay? But remember, this is for the whole farm."

"Yes, Mrs. Vega. I will be okay."My soul laughed at the idea of Mrs. Vega. She's so beautiful, yet her mouth is so curt. Not only that- she's full of contradictions: 'Be serious and focus, but be happy and relaxed?' *How could I relax? I think that I just found my soul mate...if they exist,*

and I'm not even sure if he likes me like that.

C'mon, you know he likes you. Why would he

pursue you?

Well, it doesn't matter now because I'm not at our

spot, and he probably doesn't think I like him. I guess that's

why life sucks because no matter how much you love

someone, the shit never works out. There is always some

cosmic force that makes you two seconds late from finding

your love and truly being with them.

Jade, that's bullshit! You want him. You find a way

to make him yours.

The inner voices resonating the internal struggle in

my heart were drowned out by the sound of the second

bell ringing. I raced down the hall, partly because I didn't

want to get another tardy slip and risk detention, but the

other part, the bigger part, was because I loved him. I

knew I wanted to spend every waking second with him, even if it was for just a walk down the hall. I didn't see him that day. But I was with him.

6

The next day, I was feverish. I wanted so badly to see Tony. I played loud and proud in fifth period. I made sure not to miss any notes. Mrs. Vega commended my playing and attributed it to our pep talk. I wrapped my violin up in warp speed, and ran out the door. Our school was painted in orange and blue to celebrate homecoming. *Oh shit. Homecoming is here! I hope he asks me to the dance. I hope... Oh there he is. Quit running. Okay. Act cool. Oh shit. I don't know if I can do that, but I'll try. KEEP COOL.*

I walked by passed the orange lockers and saw him standing there. His eyes met mine and held me captive. He walked passed his friends towards me. My knees were wobbling. My heart was filled with fear.

29

C'mon Jade. Get it together. This guy was a nerd to you a week ago. What the hell happened? He hasn't even kissed you yet. Play it cool.

"Wassup, Jade?" *DAMN IT! Why is he always so damn sure of himself?*

"Nothing. I'm just headed to class." *Yes, that was cool. Wasn't it? Cool. Yes.*

"So you're too cool to say hi now? I thought we were good. I missed you yesterday."

"Missed?" I emphasized.

"Yes, missed. You're pretty cool, Jade. So I thought I would let you into my presence."

I belted out a loud laugh. "Why, Mr. Georgino? You got humor. I believe it's been the other way around. You're lucky to be in *my* presence." *God, I love his banter. He's so witty. He's so challenging.*

"So whadya say?" He teased.

"As to what?" I inquired.

"As to going to the movies, finally." He tossed his hair out of his face. Maybe he needed a haircut. Either way, I thought it was the cutest thing. That's the funny thing about love- you take into account all of the other person's funny idiosyncrasies. It might be annoying later, but it's cute as hell when you first fall in love.

"Wow, I think that's homecoming weekend, and I have plans," I lied. I hated *watching* football and had no desire to go to the game. I didn't even care if it was my senior year. I just didn't like watching it. Now, playing football was fun and a different story. Tony was a different story too- hopefully, my story.

"I know for a fact that you don't like football. And as for plans, they don't matter if I'm not in them."

"I like playing football!" I protested. "Wait. So you've been checking on me?" *Yes, he's been checking on*

31

me! He likes me. He really likes me. My heart was racing. It was already at 60 miles per hour and now it's doing the Indy 500. *I'm really fucked. Should I tell him how I feel?*

NO! Don't tell him. Play it cool. "Okay," I gave in.

"Great, let's go after school because your momma and your neighborhood scare me."

"Whatever, that didn't stop you from going to get me, did it?" I asked him defiantly.

No, I'm not one of those girls that are just worth whatever is between her legs. You gotta get to my mind to get me.

"Well, let's just say that some things in life are worth it." His eyes turned dark, but his grin was wide, and I detected the hint of sincerity and seriousness in his words. We parted our separate ways into our individual classes. *Damn, I think he has me. Fuck.*

7

Tony picked me up a little late the following

Saturday afternoon. I was going through the changes

waiting for him too. I felt scared shitless. I was scared that

he was getting bored with me. After all, I'm not a

comedian. How long could I keep up this witty banter? I

was scared because maybe he didn't want me anymore.

No you're crazy. Who doesn't want you?

Nevertheless, he picked me up. We drove from the

Westside to some Southside mall. I had no idea where we

were. Other than orchestra recitals, my momma didn't

"let" me out much.

My momma thought she was keeping me safe, I

guess. I never understood how she could have thought she

was keeping me safe. Every day on my way to school, I

walked passed crack heads, dope boys, and men who

leered at me with lust in their eyes. The whole

neighborhood imploded around us, and yet for some reason she was keeping me safe by refusing to let me kick it in safer neighborhoods. *Whatever, one day I will travel so far on my own that she'll question my existence. How's that for not being "let out"?*

Tony and I pulled up to the deserted parking lot. The mall really looked like it had seen better days. I imagined it being a magnificent structure at one time, full of people and happy shoppers. Now it looked like a mere ghost in a shell- depleted and worn down. But you couldn't tell me that it was a dump then. I would've thought I was at Disneyland thanks to the pure happiness that I felt in my heart. I was with Tony!

I was with Tony, and my heart was beating faster than an Olympic runner before the sounds of the gunshot. I was on cloud nine and trying so desperately not to show it. It was Fall and 64 degrees outside, but it felt like mid

July. I prayed that he didn't notice. And he didn't. He looked at me every now and then and gave me this wry smile- a smile that I would be captivated by for the rest of my life.

My heart jumped three beats. *When da fuck did this happen? Why am I so happy to be with this dude?* Tony took me by the hand and pulled me across the street. He was being protective of me. I felt that he really liked me- hopefully more than I liked him. Love is wonderful, but it can be a dangerous weapon when one person likes the other one a little more.

We went to the box office, and he bought our tickets. He was an absolute gentleman. Something about him seemed a little too good to be true. He probably had some wicked side of him. Maybe he tortured animals for fun. I didn't care if he did. I was hooked on how he treated me, and he treated me like a queen.

35

We took our seats, sat down, and watched some boring action-comedy, Hollywood trash. I think I could have counted the jokes that really made me laugh on one hand- possibly one finger. It probably would have received a Rotten Tomatoes score of 50%, no 45%. It was just that mediocre. But I still had the best time of my life.

I had the most wonderful time because of what happened after the movie. We walked outside on our way to the car. My head must have been so high in the clouds because I could not see the menacing cracks in the concrete secretly plotting my demise ahead. Because I didn't want to look too tomboyish, I wore my heels. The heels and my lack of expertise in wearing them, in conjunction with the malevolent cracks in the street, led up to my downfall. Before I knew it, I was heading towards the ground fast. Yet, somehow, my face didn't smash on the concrete.

I was doubly embarrassed. I was embarrassed for falling, but I was also embarrassed for where I landed. I landed right into Tony's arms! It was such a cliché trip and fall that could have only happened in a Carry Grant or Rock Hudson movie. I literally fell right into that boy's arms. My face beamed with embarrassment, but his face pictured extreme delight. *Damn, he's fast and strong.*

Tony paused and held onto me as if he was protecting a valuable vase from shattering. I looked down at myself and realized that my heart was pumped full of adrenaline from both the act of falling and from embarrassment. However, that same organ raced with a new feeling- hope. I was hoping- no, wishing, that Tony would kiss me, but he didn't. He held onto me in a warm embrace as he brought me to my feet. I longed for his kiss, but as the days went on, I also longed for his embrace. I felt safe, as though the world could not touch or hurt me.

Tony was my human blanket, and I was absolutely enamored with it. *But why didn't he kiss me? I guess I will never know.*

8

Sunday went on forever. I neglected my homework. I had a paper due, a book to read, a report to write, and a science project to complete. Yet, everything was "no bueno". The only thing that kept my feet grounded, and kept me from floating out of the ionosphere, were my chores and my violin. Tony holding me so close that day fortified the new love I had in my heart.

After I finished the laundry, the cooking, and the cleaning, I raced to my violin. This new love incited a fiery passion in my soul. The energy was overwhelming, and I found myself bound up like a bull in a pen. The only way I could think to release this energy was in my bow. I held my

38

violin in my arms- closely and gingerly like he held me- and started playing Gershwin's *Rhapsody in Blue*.

The beautiful melody embraced me almost like his arms. I played with ferocity, with passion, with mysticism. I took all of the longing I felt for him and put it in the small space between my bow and strings. *Mrs. Vega would have loved to hear me play like this. Maybe I will be able to play like this tomorrow if he's there.*

9

I jumped out of bed. I showered quickly, brushed my teeth, grabbed my violin, and ran out the door. I was early for the bus- too early and had to wait impatiently for twenty minutes. Twenty minutes in the pouring, freezing rain holding onto a book bag and a violin case with barely enough light outside to see down the street. It was not a good way to start the day. I even forgot to eat, and hunger pains started rising in my stomach. Infuriated by my lack of self care, I started berating myself *to myself.*

Look Jade. Who do you think you're fooling? You ain't fooling nobody. You got here early to see this dude, didn't you? Look, baby J. You can't live off love. You gotta eat- even if it's just a little something. Just eat- anything. You're gonna collapse if you don't, and Romeo ain't here to catch you this time.

I looked around for an open store and saw a bodega on the corner that I never noticed before. The sign read that it was open. I walked inside, and the man standing behind the register looked at me. His initial examination was one of distrust. This was short lived as I saw a perverted smirk begin to creep from one end of his face to the other.

"Aren't you up a little too early, sweetheart?" His body posture changed, too.

"No," I replied curtly. Something about the way this guy was looking at me made me feel that I wasn't a girl to the world anymore. I was a woman and possibly an object to be lusted after.

But you feel that lust too, don't you, Jade?

Damn it, why didn't he kiss me? I want him so badly that I'm beating the sun to school. I hope he kisses me today before I go insane. Is he gay? NO. He looks at you like the guy standing behind the register- just a lot less creepy.

I paid for my Snickers bar and Coke and ran as fast as I could out of that store. If I hadn't, maybe I would have been kidnapped and placed in some obscure harem on the Westside of Chicago.

A relief came over my spirit as I hurriedly ate my breakfast of champions. My belly thanked me, too. I was living off of my euphoric love and accompanying energy that I kept forgetting to eat. I gulped down the soda because I had the metabolism of an eight year old and sighed with relief as I noticed that the sun was finally making its appearance and my bus was coming around the corner. *Hopefully, the freaks that came out at night have retreated, especially that creepy bodega guy.*

I raced to the school, which was scary and unusual because I hated going to school, and not because I was a bad student. I didn't like school much because I was bored with it. I was in my last year of high school, and I was ready to move onto bigger and better things. I didn't have time for math, science, reading, or writing. All I had time for was my music. All I wanted time for was him.

I arrived at the school gates with the early period people. Some of them looked at me like they had never seen me before, which I'm sure they hadn't. Although I was a senior, I hated going to school early. I was a late

riser, and definitely not an early bird, so I didn't take
classes that started at the butt crack of dawn. I only had
one class that began that early, and I ended up dropping
the class after the teacher told me to drop it.

"Jade, darling, you've already missed ten classes. If
you stay enrolled, I'm going to have to fail you," I
remember Mrs. Kennedy telling me. If there was one thing
that got under my skin to the point that it absolutely
maddened me, it was failure. I hated failing. It bothered
my spirit more than anything, and because of that, I
dropped the class. I hated math, and I hated getting up
early, so dropping the class was a win-win for me. Yet, I
was early today.

Instead of making it to an early class on time;
today, I was early because I committed Tony's schedule to
my long-term memory. I knew that I would have a few
minutes to see him before he started class, and maybe

43

steal our first kiss. But to my surprise, he wasn't there today.

I looked for him in the halls between classes. Each time the bell rang to end class, my heart fluttered with the hope of seeing him. Each time the second bell rang, my heart dropped when I didn't see his brown hair and blue eyes walking towards me. I was absolutely devastated when I realized that he was not coming to school today.

My focus shifted from pursuit of Tony to paying attention in class. My floating head became grounded quickly after I realized that the paper I put off working on this weekend was due in three days. After class was over, I hustled to the library and raided the shelves for the books that I needed to complete the assignment.

I left my violin at school in my locker and loaded the books between my back-pack and my hands. I was a little over a buck twenty, and the weight from the books

44

swayed me back and forth like a ship at high seas. I liked

Tony. No, I loved Tony, but greater than my love for Tony

was the fear of failure if I did not turn in that assignment.

Why? Because fuck failure.

I trudged slovenly to the bus stop, got on, and

looked out the window, watching the sun set on the

horizon.

Jade, you miss him. You actually missed someone.

I looked out the window and smiled as I watched

the people go about their lives in the chilly autumn

weather.

10

The next day I slowly rolled out of bed. I dragged

my feet to the bathroom. I brushed my teeth so slowly that

I could count each brush stroke. I put on my clothes with

less enthusiasm, ate with less enthusiasm, and headed out

the door leaving those heavy books behind, also with less enthusiasm.

The euphoric high of love caught up with my metabolism and my late night paper cram writing, and moved my body in retrograde. I went to school. I attended class. I played my violin with less passion in orchestra. I simply existed. I also forgot to eat again.

When the bell rang, I bee lined it for the vending machines. I put my seventy-five cents in and pressed that heavenly combination that granted me a Snickers bar. As I bent over to retrieve my chocolate prize, I heard a familiar voice say, "Be careful. Don't trip this time."

Suddenly, I didn't want the Snickers. *What Snickers? In my teamsters voice.* I had a big smile on my face and suddenly my wariness evaporated.

"Thank you for your concern," I said, smiling wide now.

"Well, I wasn't feeling well after we left each other Saturday. I got sick, and my mom made me stay home, but..."

"Yes?" I inquired hanging onto every word. "But, what?"

"But I missed you," he said sheepishly.

"Aww, You missed me?" I asked bewildered, embarrassed, and shocked that he could assert such a truth. *He's so damn sure of himself, isn't he? Just like you. But you missed him, too. Tell him. Tell him that you missed him and that you got to school unnaturally early to see him?!*

"Thank you. I noticed that you weren't here, and I got a little worried."

Wuss!

"Well, I'm here now. You're here now. So what do you say?" His eyes were sparkling and giddy.

"I say that I am very tired. I got up too early yesterday, and went to bed too late. I have this paper due in two days, and I haven't started writing yet- just reading. I didn't even play my violin well today. So I say that I am just going to go home and go to bed, and then get up and write."

Tony looked away. He seemed almost disappointed that he could not spend any time- with me. He cocked his head and smiled. "Well, when you're done being a slacker, I'm going to take you to one of my favorite spots."

I laughed, "Okay." He took my candy bar out of the machine and handed it to me. "By the way, these are really bad for you."

"So now you're concerned about my well-being?" I playfully snapped.

"Just a little. No more than you being worried about me being gone," he laughed.

Touché, my love. Well, at least he can read between my lines, which is good enough for me.

We walked down the hall holding hands. He leaned over and kissed my lips. It was our first kiss! My heart imploded before the second bell rang, and we departed. I watched him walk away until he was a mere impression on my mind. *Damn, girl. You got it bad. Hook. Line. And sinker.*

"I think I could love him forever," I whispered so softly that no one around me could hear, but also so permanently that my words were imprinted on the walls forever.

11

Fall rolled into the holiday season. I was both looking forward to the holidays and dreading it as well. I was excited because the holiday season meant more performances and more recognition, and possibly more scholarships to schools I could only dream of attending. I loved playing my violin all over the city. Our group didn't get paid because we were kids in a high school entity, but I loved playing at the churches and fancy hotels anyway. I loved being out in the world and playing for people... not family or judges at the contests, but actual people who had likes and dislikes, people who had actual opinions and could tell you whether they like your music as opposed to people blowing steam up your ass.

Although I was only seventeen, I wasn't born yesterday. I knew that it was easy for people to get caught up in the fact that I was a poor black girl from Chicago's worst ghetto neighborhood, playing classical music. People were just mystified that I could play a coveted instrument

like the violin. Those were the people that wasted my
time.

I was an artist! I played my violin with the intent
to craft my art and hone my skills. I didn't play for people
to have internal conflicts with their inner racist beliefs. I
played because it was in my soul to play, and I didn't have
time for empty, hollow, and racist compliments. The
people who walked up to me to tell me that I was
gorgeous were okay, too. But don't give me a compliment
because I am a black girl playing classical music. I had no
time for that!

This year the gigs were plentiful. I played at the
Hilton, the Sheraton, and the Daley Center. I played at
various churches and schools. My biggest joy was playing
at schools and seeing the looks on young girls' faces.
Maybe after seeing me play, they felt that they could do it,
too. I loved empowering the young ones. My belief was

that you should make your destiny your bitch. You make
things happen- not the other way around.

However, this year was different. My art was
getting stronger. I could feel the notes leave my heart and
enter my listeners' ears. I was a different player- a soulful
one. Even Mrs. Vega complimented me once or twice
about my playing. I could hear her shrill voice floating in
my mind's ear, "You're becoming quite the formidable
player, now." *What happened?*

Jade, you know what happened.

This season was different because I met him...
because I loved him. All of the gigs were nice. I loved the
traveling, meeting new people, and hearing the wonderful
compliments about my craft, but when I was there- he
wasn't. Every recital, every gig, and every rehearsal took
the only time that I had to give him.

I found myself panicking and was overwhelmed with fear. I didn't want to lose him. He was mine, and I felt like I was his. My heart dropped as I thought about all of the chicks lining up to be with him. In reality, they weren't actually there lining up to be with him, but you couldn't tell my mind or my heart that. I heard scores of high school girls' voices rolled into one voice. They all chanted, "She's gone. Let's get him", "She's gone. Let's get him", over and over again. I shuttered and was defeated at the idea of losing him.

My palms were sweaty, my heart dropped three octaves, and I found myself falling into a transcendental pit. I was overwhelmed with doubt. I felt in my spirit that he was so wonderful, and I wasn't wonderful enough to keep him "entertained" or "interested". Sooner, rather than later, some prettier girl would come around and take him, and I would be the girl who lost her yellow little basket. A tisket a tasket.

The idea of failing to keep his love washed over me like acid rain onto a tree. It started to destroy my outer layers- leaving only the exposed vulnerable ones. My heart sank. My stomach bubbled. My head became feverish. I started to drift away like a lost kite in an endless wind.

A fire deep inside of me ignited. This fire configured itself into a lioness that took on a raspy, serious voice. It belted out a loud roar and told me: *Do not lose yourself in this love. Use this love to become better and stronger, but do not lose yourself. You are wonderful and one of a kind. He knows this. You make your own destiny. His love does not make you who you are.*

I smiled. The lioness retreated inside of me. I picked up my bow and played with ferocity and passion for the rest of the holiday season.

12

Christmas time was enchanting. For the first time, I was in love. I felt like I had the world on a string. I was even singing at the top of my lungs, too. Frank Sinatra, Lady Day, Anita, Aretha, and Whitney had nothing on me. I was in love, and I wasn't afraid to show it.

My girlfriends saw the twinkle in my eyes. They also saw the kisses that Tony stole from me in the halls between classes. They knew it. I knew it. Everyone knew it. Even Mrs. Vega kept telling me to get my head into the sheet music and out of the damn clouds. But I didn't care. The only thing- person- I cared about was Tony.

Tony was in my heart and in my soul. He made me happy. Hopefully, I made him happy, too. Everyone knew I loved that boy except Tony. I couldn't bring myself to say it to him. I was partly embarrassed, partly clueless, but mostly fearful. I dreaded the idea of forming my lips to say the truth that my spirit knew too well. I could not say, "I love you."

I wanted so badly to tell him that I love him. I was brave enough to shout it from the mountains, but not brave enough to tell him to his face. I wanted to tell him how I loved being in his arms. I wanted to say how I love having him near me. I want to utter how the sound of his voice makes my knees weak. I wanted to tell him a million clichés of love. Yet, I just couldn't bring myself to tell him the most important cliché- I love you.

I would start to form the words when we would be alone. I would press my lips together in the hopes of saying it when the sun shined on his hair and definitely when his eyes sparkled like diamonds. But every time we met, all I could say was "hello". When we parted, all I could say was "goodbye".

I was dumbfounded that I was so scared. I went out like a chump every time. I imagined him saying that he loved me, too. I dreaded him saying that we were too young to be in love. Still, I needed to tell him that I loved him before winter break started and we would part ways for two weeks. I needed to make a claim on my destiny. I needed to make my mark on his heart.

The last day before winter break, I mustered up the courage to walk over to him. He was leaning against a locker talking to one of his friends.

"Hey Jade. How's it going?" he said to me. He turned to his friends and told them that he would chill later. He grabbed my hand and walked me outside. It was the end of the day. It was now or never.

Even in the cold, my palms were dripping with sweat. My heart was pounding inside of my chest. I turned to him and said, "Tony, I have something important to tell you, and I don't know how you are going to take it."

"What is it?" He seemed worried.

Oh my god. I don't want him to be worried. Just say it, stupid.

"Tony, I love you!" I blurted out. "I said, I love you," with a little more finesse and softness in my voice. He paused and my heart filled with fear as I thought I was the biggest jackass in history. I wanted to abort this mission and eject myself to the nearest bus stop so that I could depart from this fucked up situation. The silence was maddening. *Run... just run as fast as you can. Maybe he will forget you ever said it.*

"I'm so sorry. I'm sorr-" My apologies were cutoff as fast I had said them, and as fast as I said "I love you", Tony's tongue was down my throat. My face was in his palm. A tear was down my cheek. My forehead was feverish.

He didn't say he loved me back. He didn't have to. I was his. He was mine. I was bursting with happiness on a cellular level. We parted ways, but I kept wondering: Did he love me, too?

Jade, you know he never reciprocated it, right?

"Shut up," I told myself. "Do shut up. It doesn't matter if he doesn't love me. He kissed me after I said it to him. That was the best Christmas present ever."

13

Christmas Eve was harder this year. Momma was working late and depended on me to do almost all of the cooking. I also had to clean and watch my younger siblings. I was ten years older than my youngest sibling. Thus, while my momma worked, I cleaned and cooked and told tales of Santa. I loved Santa because it was a great way to have my younger brothers do chores for nothing. Well, it wasn't just for nothing. My brothers did have a boatload of presents hidden away in my bedroom closet. They were mounted up so high that it brought tears to my eyes- not because we had presents this year, but because I had to wrap them.

I loathed wrapping presents, but nevertheless my mother made me do it. Last year, we ran out of Christmas paper, and I suggested that we just leave them unwrapped. No- not my momma. Momma took the Chicago Tribune's Christmas Eve edition and used that. I was so annoyed, but I guess it taught me to make a way out of no way. Little did I know that lesson would get me further than I could ever imagine.

For some reason, this year was different. The workload was the same as the previous years. I was always in the kitchen dicing bell peppers and white onions for the stuffing every year like clockwork. I was always home, cleaning and scrubbing the house until I passed out from exhaustion. As always, I was up till dawn wrapping presents before my brothers came dashing into the living room, excited to see what Santa brought them this year. It sucked because I was overworked and underpaid and over exhausted, but it was Christmas break.

What made this Christmas break different is that I was going on my fourth day in a row without seeing Tony. In a little over a semester, he became unequivocally important to me. I smiled every time I saw him, even if he didn't see me. He gave me something to look forward to every time I went to school.

But four days went by, and I hadn't heard from him. No calls. No surprise visits. Nothing. It was maddening. There I stood in the school's courtyard, in the cold, and the last thing I said was that I loved him. Yes, there was a kiss... but now there was nothing but silence.

Was I too forward? Maybe I shouldn't have told him how I felt. Maybe he's scared. Maybe he thinks that I want to load him up with babies and trap him. How could he think that? He's not the only one with dreams. I have dreams, too! Damn it!

Suddenly, I jumped to my feet. The doorbell rang with perfect timing. I ran to the door desperately escaping the despair that my thoughts were propelling me towards. To my surprise, my momma was standing there holding a box in her hand.

"Who was that?" I asked. We normally did not get packages, so my despair instantly transformed into curiosity.

"I don't know," my momma said. The puzzled look on her face became deeper and more unsettling as she said, "It's for you."

"For me?" I echoed my momma's thoughts.

"Yes, open it!" she snapped impatiently. I took the package from her and walked into the living room. I sat on the sofa, placed the package onto my lap, and opened it. It was a small teddy bear and around its neck was a small shiny bracelet.

"That's cute. Who gave you that? Your father?" My momma's curiosity seemed to grow and manifested itself into her omniscient raised eyebrow.

Oh God, please don't let it be from daddy. There's only one guy that I want anything from right now, and it's not daddy.

"Read the damn card, Jade!" My mother was pointing to a small card that was hidden under tissue paper. I almost threw it away. That would have been a grave mistake for on the card said, "I feel the same way, too, from Tony".

"So who sent you the gift, baby?" My mom was at the edge of her seat, and the curiosity was driving her mad.

"Tony," I said trying so hard to muffle the smile plastered on my face. My mother's curious face went into her protective, who's trying to fuck my daughter face. "Who's Tony?" she asked dryly.

"Oh momma! You remember Tony. He was the guy that came to pick me up that day. You know, the one who didn't know you were my momma."

"That guy! I thought you got rid of him months ago."

Oh God. Please don't tell me she hates him. That would be just my luck, right?

"No, momma. Tony is my boyfriend, and I like him very very much." I defended. *Oh my God, I'm defending him. This is not going to go well.*

The deep lines in my mother's forehead became more pronounced. I knew that face. That was the "I'm worried that my daughter is going to fuck up her life" face. *Holy shit, Batman. I'm toast.*

"Your what? When did I say you could have a boyfriend?" she barked.

"The rule was when I became sixteen, I could date and have boyfriends. I'm seventeen now, momma." I defended my position, but this trial wasn't over.

"I don't like him, and I want you to get rid of him." She snapped.

"But why momma? He's nice and smart. He treats me well. Isn't that what you want for me?"

65

"But he's white. He's going to go onto college and forget about you. He's going to marry a white woman, they are going to have white children, and the world will go on. Baby, you're mysterious to him. You're exotic. He's charming. I know, but he's going to get what he wants from you. After that, he's going to leave. You're so much better than he is, baby. You've got talent, and you've got ambition. Don't throw it away to be a story he tells his friends."

Rage gathered in the back of my throat. I wanted to throw the bear and the bracelet across the room. I wanted to storm out and slam the door. I considered being his experiment, but I shortly dispelled that theory after that day on the pier. God wouldn't have made such a perfect creature just to torment me. *Right?*

Suddenly, I couldn't move. I couldn't retreat, not even to my room. I was standing in my home- paralyzed. I

66

was reduced to being nothing but a flavor of the month or call girl by my very own mother for loving someone outside of my race. I clenched my fist and found my courage. I looked into my mother's big brown eyes and said with all the conviction that I could muster, "But momma, I love him, and he's different."

"Baby, they're all different at first. Just live a little longer, and you'll see. You have power between your thighs. A power that some men will fall for, but the most powerful thing you own is in your spirit. You can't just let anyone in."

Too late, momma.

I went through Christmas Eve on autopilot. I chopped what needed to be chopped. I scrubbed what needed to be scrubbed. I wrapped all of the toys without complaint.

The next morning, my little brothers rose from their sound slumber, raced to the tree, and hastily opened all their gifts. "Jade, Jade, look what I got! Look what Santa brought us!" They cried in unison. They were beyond happy. Momma did good, and Santa remained alive for yet another year.

Yet, I envied their belief that Santa was real. I envied how something so false could ring so true in their tiny little hearts. That's the funny thing about belief systems... I guess if you truly believe in something, it becomes real. It manifests and transforms into a living breathing thing that can be appreciated by any nonbeliever. Even if that thing is something as silly as a soul mate.

As I stood with my heart in my hand, I finally understood why my momma would always stop me from telling my little brothers about Santa's true identity. I now

68

realize it's because when you shift a person's belief system, their tower comes crashing down, and that person becomes utterly lost.

My momma ruined my new version of Santa. My belief that Tony loved me evaporated as fast as it was set in stone- as fast as I opened my present. It was replaced with a perverted truth: that I was his play thing- his conquest. His love was as real as Santa Clause, and I knew his true identity- a preying wolf.

I didn't partake in our usual Christmas activities. Instead, I took my bear and my bracelet, went into to my room, pulled the covers over my head, and cried until the New Year.

14

Although ringing in the New Year erased the tears from my eyes, it didn't erase the doubt from my heart. For the first time, I doubted that Tony loved me. I doubted his smile, his eyes, and his catch phrases. I doubted myself. But, it was a new year. It was a new me. So I said, "Fuck that!"

Fuck what my mother thinks. Fuck what anybody thinks. Fuck what I think. All I know is that you would have to be a psychopath or a maniac to fake it the way he does. Something deep within came from my soul and told me: *Until he proves otherwise, love him with everything you have.*

My eyes got blurry, and I cried. But the tears that were shed were no longer of sadness. They were full of hope and promise. They were evidence of the covenant that I made with myself. I never wondered how long this promise would last, but I was going to be brave enough to see it through. Even if there is no such thing as true love; I was going to fight for my love until the end. I was going to fight until I saw the truth- the truth that Tony loved me.

15

The fourth of January could not have come fast enough. I grabbed my breakfast and ran out the door. In a hurry, I almost crushed my violin case against the door frame. Instead of leaving the house at the butt crack of dawn, I cleaned my room and completed my homework until the earth became decently lit. I arrived at school at my usual time: half past late. But I had a sense of rejuvenation.

I was going to see my man. I was going to thank my man for his beautiful gift. I was going to hold my man tight. I was going to... My heart sank as I saw him on the banister leaning over and talking to a girl. She was blonde, beautiful, and taller than me. I clenched my violin and walk towards the pair. *All is fair in love and...*

"Shut up." I told myself.

"What?" Tony said. *Oh snap. I think he heard me.*

"I didn't say anything." I lied. *Okay girlfriend. Keep it together. Keep your shit together. There is a logical explanation for this. She could be his cousin. Don't jump to conclusions. Just keep it... cool.*

"Wassup? My name is Jade, and you are?" I inquired. Tony, as if understanding what it looked like for the first time, straightened up and interjected, "This is my science partner, Sophie. We're just talking about our chemistry experiment. We're going over it today after class."

"Okay," I mumbled. *What the fuck! She's not his cousin! She's supposed to be his Goddamn cousin! What the fuck? You just tell someone you love them no less than two weeks ago and then start hanging out with Barbie over there. Fuck this shit. I stood up for our love. Oh my god. I told my momma I loved him. I told my momma! Fucking asshole... Fucki...* I started to run away. Tony caught up to me, grabbed me, held me, and kissed me.

"What's your problem?" He looked so clueless – so damn clueless.

"You and that Brittney Spears' looking chick are my problems," I snapped.

"What? That's just my lab partner. You're jealous!"

"No!" I snapped back. "I just don't like getting played." I recoiled from his embrace and was glaring at him.

"Who's playing you?"

"You are. You probably just want to get my cookies and then brag to your buddies. I'm not that kind of girl, you know? You have to earn my love."

"What? Look, I have to go, but I do *have* love for you. You do know that, right?" *He's seemed so damn sure of himself. Always so damn sure.*

"I love you too, Tony... more than I have ever loved anyone before." I whispered apologetically in his ear.

"So we're good? Then how about a kiss?" He coaxed.

"Okay." His lips pressed up to mine. The kiss lasted three seconds, but it felt like an eternity. My knees got weak, and I wanted him more.

"Tony?"

"Yes?"

"Would you be my man?"

"Who wouldn't?" He asked and walked away. I played my violin extra loud that day.

16

"Girl, who is that boy I keep seeing you with?" Kiesha's brown round eyes got bigger with curiosity.

"What boy?" I asked knowing that I didn't want to answer her question. It was just a matter of time.

"That tall boy with the hair all over his head – you know, the white one?"

I smiled when she said, "the white one". I knew who she was talking about the whole time. I just wanted to hear my best friend say it: white. They were all looking at me as if I turned my back on my race. Classmates that I had never seen or met were coming out from hallways and class room doors, glaring at me and rolling their eyes as I walked down the halls holding a white hand. It looked like it was my best friend's turn to chime in.

"Kiesha, he's my boyfriend." I said it so matter-of-factly, too, as if I was guarding the most important thing in my life- guarding my love from destruction or at least disapproving eyes.

"Jade, baby-girl, you can't be serious. That dude is corny as hell. He's too tall... too messy..."

"Too white?" I asked.

"Yes, too white. He's definitely too white."

"So, I thought love was color blind. I thought you were supposed to love someone for who they are on the inside and how they make you feel on the inside. I didn't think, or better yet know, that the condition of love depended on the pigment of their skin. Here it is, 1998... and we still think like this? What the hell is wrong with you people? Where do you see all of these so called brothers that I am "supposed to be with"?

Kiesha nodded her head disapprovingly as she shrugged.

"Well none of these dudes were checking for me or trying to holler at me. None of them were checking for me at all. Now, I got this nice guy who holds my hand, holds my books, challenges me, and makes me feel like a person and not an object, and instead of seeing a girl in love, you guys just see a person who is 'turning her back on her race'? What the hell is wrong with you all, especially you? You're supposed to be my best friend!"

Before I knew it, I stormed off. I left Kiesha in the hallway holding her black Coach purse and her mouth in her hand while I entered my fifth period English class. I had never spoken to anyone like that before. I was the friendly girl. I was the girl who tried so desperately to see the glass half full. I wasn't the warrior girl, unless someone threatened my little brothers or those I love. I wasn't the

77

girl that stood up for my convictions- maybe in writing- but definitely not out loud. Not in person. I was on fire.

I knew what Kiesha meant. It was the same thing my momma told me on Christmas. It was the same thing that my classmates' disapproving eyes said as they walked passed Tony and me in the halls. Their eyes said: "Who do you think you are with this white guy? He's white. You're black. Can't you tell?" *Well, fuck that. Who says I cannot be with this guy? What if I want to travel the world and love any man or woman that comes my way? Why do people insist on shoving me into these roles? First gender. Now race. Life doesn't make sense.*

"Ms. Jade? Ms. Jade?" *Crap, the teacher is saying something, and I totally missed it.*

"I'm sorry, Mrs. Willington, can you repeat the question?"

"Were you not paying attention in class, Ms. Jade?"

"Actually, I was, but I missed the end of your question?" *Liar! You know that Kiesha pissed you off, and you have no idea what she asked.*

"Well, Ms. Jade, I was asking what you thought about Holden Caulfield. You know, our main character in the *Catcher in the Rye?* You have read it? It was our assigned reading." The whole class turned to watch Ms. Know-It-All squirm in her boots.

"Lost." I said, in an 'I really don't give a fuck about this class' attitude.

"Excuse me. Ms. Jade?"

"I said that he's lost. He doesn't know where he belongs, but he desperately wants to belong somewhere."

"Why that is very profound, Ms. Jade. Class I want you to turn to page fifty…."

What a profound cunt. She did all that shit to embarrass me, and I still got the answer right, without doing all of the reading. I got that from the first fucking chapter. What is wrong with these teachers? It's like they want you to be upset about some extra shit, even if you have a bunch of other shit that you're already upset about. And most likely that's the shit that they don't give a fuck about.

Jade, what are you really upset about?

I'm fucking upset that I love someone that everyone says I can't love. How about that for shits and giggles?

My busy mind locked my eyes onto the classroom window. A pigeon rested on the ledge. That's one thing Chicago will not run out of: pigeons. This pigeon had its head nestled into its body. The cold did it to the bird. The cold made it retreat into itself. *I wish I could retreat into myself and disappear sometimes. Lucky bastard.*

"Ms. Jade?"

"Yes, Mrs. Willington?" *Oh God, give me strength.*

17

My fingers became callous from plucking the strings again and again. I didn't know what Mrs. Vega's problem was. We just won a competition, and now we got these city gigs. I would not have cared had my fingers not felt like they were about to fall off. My shoulder and neck hurt from keeping the instrument there for hours...

HOURS!

I'm supposed to be a senior. I'm supposed to be kissing Tony under the stairway, but no...not me. I'm playing... playing for Mrs. Vega, Chicago Public Schools, but most importantly: my future. I swear before GOD and all

81

that's up in heaven that I will NOT be a street performer. People are going to pay to see me. That's a promise.

In the meantime, I wish I didn't have these calluses. Tony had begun to notice. He stopped holding my hands as my practice time increased. I wish I could see him, hold him... kiss him. I would rather spend my time with him than with any other person in the world right now. I would rather...

"Ms. Jade?" Mrs. Vega stopped our recital with her signature shriek. Her long black hair was gathered into a tight bun. Her gaze was cold and icy and looking directly at me. *Can she hear what I'm thinking? Nah.*

"Yes, Mrs. Vega?" I nervously asked. *I think she can hear what I am thinking.*

"Ms. Jade. Can you please focus on your sheet music, your violin, and not that boy?!"

"Mrs. Vega, I am not thinking about a boy," I lied.

82

"Ms. Jade. I do not appreciate you lying to me. Stop thinking about that boy. Start thinking about excellence. Excellence waits for no one. Boys will be there. I promise. Everyone, let's continue on the count of three."

I can't believe her. It's like she's scary... "One..." *psychic... or am I that...* "Two..." transparent... "Three! Play, Ms. Jade. Play for excellence! He will be there tomorrow."

Maybe he will be, but my shoulder and fingers sure won't.

18

I thought my senior year would be easier than this. I'm exhausted. My mom won't let up on my chores or babysitting, and I have a million and one things to do. First, I have to train the freshman newbies with their violin skills. *Why did I agree to this? Oh, because of my college application.* Second, I'm playing free gigs throughout all of Chicago. Well at least the city is feeding us. *Why did I do*

83

this? Oh, because of college. Third, I'm busting my ass to get A's. *Why am I doing this? College! Holy shit, Jade. You forgot to apply to college. F-U-C-K!*

I dropped my violin, books, and Tony, too. Well, I'll only intended to drop Tony for a little while. I'm definitely going to pick him up again. I ran to my counselor, and asked for applications. She gave them to me, and then told me the major deadlines for most schools were February 21st- three weeks away. I darted for the library. I didn't want to be the one left behind in the ghettos of Chicago while watching all of my friends, including Tony, move on to bigger and better things. I wanted to be one of those bigger and better things.

I dropped the college applications down on the table. I quickly filled out the identifying information. I then moved onto SAT/ACT scores. I left that section blank for my counselors to fill out. Essay portion: check. The fabulously mean Mrs. Willington forced us to do an essay for college admission applications. *It's amazing that something she assigned to us was actually useful.* Now all I have to do is request my transcripts and send this $100 application fee? *What-da-Fuck? I can't afford this. My mom won't give me this! What am I going to do? Read the fine print, Jade. Look: waivers!*

I ran back to my counselor's office. "Ms. Cho?"

"Yes, Jade?"

"The fees for the applications are too expensive. I read something on the college application about a waiver. Can you help me with that?"

"Sure. You're one of the few people that caught that. Sit down in my office. I have to ask you some questions to see if you will qualify for it. Close the door behind you."

"Okay. Thank you." I rushed into Ms. Cho's small office, closed the door behind me, and sat down. Her office was covered with student files, but on the walls were beautiful flowers drawn in pencil. I looked at the bottom corner for the artists' name. It said "Cho". Ms. Cho ignored my bewilderment in her beautiful art, and sat down at her computer.

"No worries, Jade. First, how many people live in your household?"

"Five."

"Okay, how much money do your parents make per month?"

"Four thousand dollars at her first job, and then I think she makes an extra fifteen hundred at her second job?"

"So five thousand five hundred dollars a month?"

"Yes."

"Before or after taxes?"

"She makes that money after taxes, I think."

"Does your father work, too?"

"Yes, but he is not in my household. My parents are divorced."

"Do you know how much he makes?"

"No."

"No worries. I will just enter this information using your mother's income only. That might work out for you."

This is not going to be good. I can feel it.

"Unfortunately, based off what you told me, you are ineligible for the waiver, Jade."

"What does that mean, Ms. Cho?"

"Well, Jade, that means that we can't help you with your college application fees. Your mom makes too much money for you to qualify for the waiver."

I knew it. Don't cry.

I got up to leave her office. "Okay, well thanks for checking, Ms. Cho. I really appreciate that." *Fuck. Now what are you going to do? You know your mom is just going to say that she can't afford it, and the deadline is in three weeks! Just walk out the door and don't cry.*

"Jade?"

"Yes?" I turned around, grateful that no tears escaped my eyes.

"Jade, if you're worried about paying for college fees, you might want to check into scholarships and financial aid. Did you fill out a FAFSA form?"

"What is a F-A-F-S-A?" I asked.

"Ms. Jade, a FAFSA form is an application for federal financial aid. They pay the school on your behalf so that you can go to college. Unlike primary and secondary public education, post-secondary education is not free. College can be very expensive. So you should try to get

88

some grants, scholarships, and loans to pay for your investment. The FAFSA form tells the school what types of aid you are eligible for. Grants and scholarships are wonderful because you don't have to pay them back. Loans, however, you must pay back. But we won't know anything until you fill out a FAFSA. It is very important. Furthermore, if school application fees are too expensive for you, I recommend that you pick two colleges that you really like and bet on those." Ms. Cho handed me a pile of papers that read: FAFSA.

"Thanks. Wow, that's a lot to take in… especially since I didn't know about this a second ago." I said hopelessly.

"Well, Jade, it is like I always say: a best defense is a great offense, and you can't strategize without knowledge. You found out a few heavy things today. So let's see what you do with it. Okay?"

"Thanks, again... for everything." I started to walk out the door again. My hear weighed heavy, and it showed on my face.

"Jade?" I turned around, and this time one single tear ran down my cheek. I couldn't control it. I didn't even want to. My life's destiny depended on money that I knew my mother would not give me, and I couldn't get it from anywhere else.

"Jade?" Ms. Cho called again as if she heard my despair.

"Yes, Ms. Cho?"

"Remember, nothing in this world worth having is easy to come by. Nothing. If you want something, if you really want it, you may suffer. But that suffering makes the thing that you want most so worthy of having. Believe in yourself, dear. You can do anything. I've watched you, and

I am very good at making assessments in people. It's why they pay me the big bucks."

"Thank you, Ms. Cho." I whispered and walked away.

19

After speaking to Ms. Cho, I rushed home from school- partly because I did not have rehearsal that day, and partly because I wanted to catch my mom before she left for her night shift at work. I left everything at school. I left my violin, my books, and Tony. I bolted from the bus after the doors opened at my stop. I was determined. I ran two blocks with my coat open. My chest was exposed to the ice cold winter elements, and my heart was opened to possibilities. Ms. Cho was right. I was determined.

I wouldn't let the ghetto be my final resting place. If college was going to be my way out, I was going to make sure that I played the game. I ran up the steps and burst through the door. I was determined. My mother was going to hear me out, and she would not say no.

Oh my God, what if she says no? Well, I will ask dad. What if he says no? Then I will take up a collection.

"Momma... momma!"

"What?!"

"Momma, I have to ask you something."

"Okay, go ahead."

"I am applying for two colleges, and I need money for the application fee. I asked about a waiver so I would not have to pay, but they told me that you make too much money."

"Well, how much you need?"

"I need one hundred dollars per application in a cashier's check in two weeks."

"Well, I'll see what I can do."

Oh Lord, I know what that means. It means you're not going to get it. You better try a different approach.

"Mom, the college deadline is in two weeks. If I don't get that money in, I won't be able to go to college next school year."

"Why didn't you say that? I will get it for you tomorrow. My baby is not going to miss out on school."

"Thanks momma. I also need you to fill out this FAFSA form so that I can get financial aid to pay for school once I get accepted into college."

"When is that due, Jade?"

"I don't know the exact due date, mom."

"I'll see what I can do!"

Fuck! I should have just given her the same date. Well at least I can pay to play, and I'm in it to win it!

20

I didn't get March in Chicago. On the school front, everything was calm. The competitions and gigs were done, my college applications were turned in, and senioritis has officially set in. But the weather was anything but calm. The winter had turned into something ferocious. The wind was howling. The snow was deep. The air was so cold that not only can you see your breath, but you can also see the icicles that formed around it. I hated the cold so much, but why I hated it was for a completely different reason.

I didn't hate the cold because you couldn't feel your toes in your boots. I didn't hate the cold because the drafts would go inside your coat and take possession of your spinal cord. I didn't hate the cold because it took a whole day for your body to warm up, just in time for you to go back outside. No, I hated the cold because I could not see Tony.

The cold meant that Tony wouldn't wait for me to get out of my last class. The cold meant that he would go straight home. The cold meant that it was painful for our lips to touch outside, and I wanted his lips. I wanted more of him, but it was too damn cold to do that or anything else.

On days like that, I would think that he would forget me. I would fear that he would forget our love. I was too stupid and naïve and thought that all of the world's love could be secured when two lips touched. Yet, if those lips do not meet or if one set of lips were meeting someone else's while the other person is still in class, then... that's why I fucking hated the cold. Fuck the cold.

21

Thank God April came! The winter season was maddening. I was overworked, underpaid, and under loved. Tony stopped meeting me at our places. He stopped holding my hand. He stopped kissing me. He just stopped. I didn't think anything of it because I was so busy with college applications and my recitals.

Was I too busy for him? Nah.

Tony was busy, too. He was on the basketball and wrestling teams. He worked. He had a family, too. We're both busy, right?

Oh no, what if you're just his high school pet, and he's conditioning himself for his college life- a life without you?

Nah. I'm too fly. Right?

Panic and insecurity overwhelmed me, and I could not breathe. I had one objective: find Tony. I did. I saw him, but he didn't see me. I saw him standing by his

friends. His head was cocked back. His hair was brown and

bouncy.

Aw he's so cute. But he's got his boys with him. You

don't want to be that 'needy' girlfriend do you?

No.

Then play it cool. Play it cool!

Yes. I'm playing it... cool.

I walked by him as cool as I could. I didn't speak,

but I let my eyes do the talking. I waived hello to the group

as I walked by. I was praying that he would leave them,

and he did.

See. I knew he loved me.

"Jade?" Tony called.

Just keep walking. Let him call you a second time.

"Jade?!" I stopped and turned around.

In the sexiest voice I could muster, I said, "Yes, Tony?"

"Whadya say? I haven't seen you around in a long time."

"Yeah, I was wondering about that, too. You don't love me no more?"

"Me not love you? You're the one I can't get a hold of because you're always gone somewhere or playing at some place."

He's right. I have been really unavailable. It is interesting that he has still not answered the question regarding his love for me. As a matter of fact, I don't think he's ever specifically said 'I love you'.

"So it's my fault that we haven't seen each other? I've called you- a lot. Your mom always answers, and she always tells me that you are not there. So if I am the busy one, and I can take the time to call you, what's your excuse? Again, you don't love me anymore?" I asked as firmly as possible.

Holy shit, Jade. I think you're angry and dishing out some truth. You just thought he was cute a moment ago. What happened?

"Look, we're too young for love." Tony exclaimed.

"Says who?" I questioned him as seriously as a heart attack. "Look, I know that I am young, but as long as I have been alive I've always known what I wanted, what I wanted to do, and who I fucking want!"

"But people change, Jade. Things never stay the same."

Hmm, is he saying what I think he's saying. What a wishy washy motherfucker!

"True, people change, but what is in your heart never changes. When I say I love someone, it's not for play. It's forever." I defended my stance for as long as I could.

"But we're so young, Jade. How do you know?"

"Because I am amazing… because I just do. I don't why I know I love you, but I just do. It's like being born. You don't know what to do to be born. You're just born. That's how love is for me. I just love. I know when it's right. I know when it's wrong. You're like my magnet. I didn't want it to be that way, but it just is.

"Jade, this is too much for me."

Is he saying what I think he's saying? I'd just wish he'd fucking say it already.

"What are you saying?"

Oh girl, you better brace yourself.

"What I am saying is that I think you're a great girl, but not for me. Besides we come from two different worlds, and its better this way for us. You're going to go on in life and do great things, and we'll still be friends. I promise."

His brain must be synced with my momma's. What the fuck?! I'm being dumped? But I really love him. I don't want to be just a fucking friend. I can't be his friend. It hurts too fucking much.

"I don't want to be your friend. I'm so stupid thinking that I found my soul mate."

"Soul mate? Jade don't be a baby. Those do not exist." Tony stated, as if he unlocked the secrets of the universe.

Great! Now he'll run off to the world and tell all the little boys and girls that Santa doesn't exist, too. You know, he's so fucking stupid. He doesn't believe in magic and romance. But I do. I guess I am the stupid one.

"Yes, they do. I feel it even if you're too stupid not to feel it. I do." I whispered defiantly.

"Stupid? Did you just call me stupid?"

"Yes Tony, you are stupid, and you can also fuck off!" I shouted. People stopped and looked up for a second, but I didn't care. I was like George H.W. Bush when he dropped bombs on Baghdad. I had zero fucks to give.

I bolted down the hall as fast as I could. I wouldn't let him see me cry. I won't let anyone see me cry... not over some dude. Fuck him.

But this isn't any 'dude' right?

Oh Jade, you can fuck off, too!

22

Thank God Tony broke my heart on a Friday. If it were any other day, I wouldn't have made it. Even worse than Tony seeing me cry would be the myriad of black young women looking at me with their stupid "I told you so" eyes rolling in the back of their heads. I couldn't take that. I think I have even seen some of the black teachers

102

warning me with their eye movements. Nope. I couldn't face them either. I'm the bravest girl I know, but fuck all that. Why give yourself unnecessary drama if you don't have to?

My mom was unusually nice to me that weekend. I didn't tell her that Tony broke my heart in a million pieces. I didn't tell her that the pieces that remained were left under his black military boots. I didn't tell her because I knew that she would hunt him down and kick the living shit out of him. But the real reason I didn't tell her was because a part of me wanted to prove her wrong.

A part of me really wanted to marry Tony and show her that I was worthy of him and his family. I wanted to show her that people do love people because of who they are on the inside and not because of their credentials on a resume or the color of their skin, hair, and eyes. Finally, I just wanted to show her that someone like him –

someone sweet and smart and challenging- could love someone like me. I needed to know that someone outside of me who was on my level thought that I was special, too. But I wasn't.

I wasn't special. I wasn't charming. I wasn't different. I was just Jade, a poor black girl from Chicago's Westside who had mediocre talent at best. I couldn't be bigger than what I was. How dare I dream of true love? What is true love? If it does exist, it is definitely for someone else to have. I should have known this because my mother told me so. She told me that I was a play thing- just a conquest.

Thank God it was cold that day, and the only warm place to go was my bed. I had an excuse for not showing my face to the world. I had a warm place that my cries and screams could escape to without anyone else hearing them. My whaling was transited to that same forest where the trees would fall without making a sound.

I cried and cried. Yet, I couldn't figure out what was worse: my mom telling me that someone like Tony wouldn't love me because I was black or Tony telling me that he couldn't love me because we were young. Maybe, I'll meet someone new, and he will tell me that he cannot love me because I am gifted.

Ha! See, Jade? Even in despair, you can still be funny. That will take you far. You've got some "bounce back".

But what good is this "bounce back" if it cannot help me now when I need it most?

I was thrown unexpectedly in the throes of depression because of one question that I really meant as a joke: "You don't love me no more?" It was a joke. Right? Because I was so sure that he loved me. I was so sure that I could bet my first born son on it. I'm great and really awesome at detecting bullshit and ulterior motives. But I couldn't find any malice in his smile or in his caress. I couldn't detect his malevolence in his kiss. I just saw love.

I pulled the covers over my head and cried from Saturday to Sunday. That bounce back I had didn't bounce back long enough to get me out of bed. Fuck this.

23

Fuck "bounce back". I needed Prozac. I managed to wipe the tears from my eyes on the following Monday morning just long enough to hide them from my family. Let's see. Getting my little brothers ready for school takes thirty minutes. Getting myself ready for school takes thirty minutes. If I could just keep my shit together for an hour, I can cry for my ten minute walk to the bus stop. If the bus is taking its usually slow ass time getting to my stop, then I can cry for an extra fifteen minutes. By the time I get on the bus, I should be all cried out. My eyes will be red, but I can tell people that I am smoking weed, and that's cool.

They won't believe you, Ms. Perfect.

Nope. They sure won't, but when has that ever stopped me from trying?

True. Good luck.

Thanks, bitch.

24

School started, and I was dreading the long walk through the hall. It felt like everyone's eyes were on me. It felt like people knew what happened. It felt like I was the subject of everyone's conversations at that very moment. That's how it felt. Yet, reality was something extremely different.

In reality, it was business as usual... or at least school as usual. Students were hanging by their lockers, cracking jokes, and avoiding class. No one looked at me.

No one talked to me. I looked up, and when I realized this, I felt that I got away from love's lost embarrassment completely Scott free. I smirked at the possibility of bringing myself from the clutches of despair. I can do this... I can do this... I can! I cannot!

Tony was standing in front of me about four locker rows down. How could I have missed him? He started walking closer to me. I did a 360 and started trucking it up the other hallway towards the opposite end of the school, which was further away from my class. Though I didn't care. I wanted to avoid Tony at all costs, but it was too late. He saw me. I knew he saw me.

So fucking what if he saw you? So what if he knows you saw him? Get the hell out of here, already! Fuck Tony!

I booked it down the hallway, and then the dreaded inevitable happened: Tony called me.

"Hey Jade. Jade, wait up." I pretended that I didn't hear him. I started walking as fast as I could while holding onto four textbooks, a purse, and a violin, which unfortunately for me was not very fast.

"Yo, Jade! Stop!" I stopped. I turned around. I put the most frightening look I could muster on my face. It wasn't as scary as one of my mother's looks- the ones that can make mountains crumble. But I am my mother's child. It was in my DNA.

"What?!" I managed to say in an equally terrifying voice. "What do you want, Tony?! I'm busy."

"Well for starters, I want to know why you are so angry. Why didn't you stop when you heard me calling you? And why did you tell me to 'fuck off'? Those are not words used by a lady."

"Well maybe I'm not a lady," I muttered.

"You are too a lady. You're my lady."

109

"I'm not your lady or anybody's lady. You made that clear on Friday. Or do you have some weird case of amnesia? Do you need medical attention? Did you bump your head?"

"What are you talking about Friday? All I said was that we were too young for love. You said we were not, and then you bolted out of here like some crazy lady."

"Are you serious? You said and I quote, 'I think you're a great girl but not for me. It's better this way. We can still be friends.' Thus, and therefore and in sum and albeit, I'm not your fucking lady! I'm not your girl! I'm not even your friend!"

"I said that?" Tony asked.

I can't believe he looks so goddamn puzzled. Where is that "I am so damn sure of myself" look now?

"Yes you did. So please excuse me. I'm running late, and I have already wasted too much of my precious

110

time." I yelled and pushed past him going the *right* way to my class. I wasn't going to truck it through a longer way just because he was the one who fucked up. Nope. I walked down the hall with my pride in my hand amongst other things. Tony took up too much of my time *and heart* already. I was not going to let him make me late to class either cause fuck that!

25

Even though my heart was broken, I enjoyed April. April meant musicals. I played my violin in all of the past musicals, but I always wanted to be on stage singing and dancing and not stuck in throes of the orchestra pit staring at sheet music under a dim shitty light. Today was going to be my day to shine. Today, I was going to sing.

The night before, I had conjured up all the vocal powers of Sinatra, Holiday, and Franklin. I was going to be awesome. I was going to breathtaking. The confidence I had even poured into my violin playing. Mrs. Vega was lifting her baton and shouting something about "excellence". But I didn't care, nor did I hear exactly what she was saying.

I didn't hear what she said because I staring at the hands of the clock while sawing my violin with my bow. With each tick and tock, I was closer to my destiny as a singer: Jade, The Singing Violinist! I could see people throwing roses on stage for me. I could feel the petals as they fell on my arms. I could smell their lovely fragrance as they were thrown from the balconies of my mind's eye. I could see... sheet music?

"Um, Mrs. Vega? What is this sheet music for, and why are you only giving it to the ensemble members?"

"My Dear Jade. It's for the musical that we are performing."

"Yes, Mrs. Vega, but why are you giving it to me?"

"Mrs. Jade. You are the first chair, right?"

"Yes, but I told you that I wanted to audition for one of the acting parts since this is my last year."

"Well, you can't play and act, Ms. Jade."

Is she laughing at you, Jade? Why is she so damn nonchalant? Can't she tell this is your future?

"Yes, I know. I can't play and act, so I just want to act this time," I said, extremely annoyed.

"Ms. Jade. You are a violinist. You play the violin. Plus, you're my first chair and the only one who can play this sheet music. Plus…"

"Mrs. Vega…"

"Plus, Ms. Jade, there will be recruiters to some of the colleges checking out the actors and the musicians. Do you really want to throw away four years of hard work for something that you might be good at?"

"But I can sing, Mrs. Vega," I pleaded for the chance of a lifetime.

"Yes, you can sing, Ms. Jade. But your violin can *si...i...ing*! Besides, do you really want to be a jack of all trades and a master of none? Your servant is the violin, Ms. Jade. You are its master. Remember that!"

"Well can I audition at least?"

"You may try, but I already told the chorus and acting directors that you would be my first chair. They will most immediately disqualify you."

Damn, I can't get anything that I want, not in love nor in life.

"Cheer up, Ms. Jade. Excellence must have its sacrifices."

Fuck excellence. I want Tony. I want to sing. Well at least it's warm enough to play football. I'd better get ready for gym.

26

"Attention class!" said Mrs. Croll, our gym instructor. All the girls stopped what they were doing and looked up at Mrs. Croll, but we weren't ready for what came next.

"Attention class. The football field will be undergoing renovations for the next few weeks so we will have to cancel the football segment of gym class."

"FUCK!"

Oh shit, I said that out loud.

"Who said that?" Mrs. Croll demanded. "Who said that? Or I swear to God that you females will be running laps for the next fifty minutes!"

"I said it! I said it because it was the only thing that I was looking forward to, and now it's gone."

"Even still Ms…. Ms…."

"Jade." *I can't believe I told her my name. Bitch didn't know who I was for the last four years.*

"Even still, Ms. Jade, that is no excuse for you to curse in class. The next outburst you have, I will send your ass to detention. Is that clear?"

"Yes, ma'am."

"Good. Now, like Jade, a lot of you will be disappointed. I must agree that I am disappointed as well, which is why I am going to teach you indoor hockey."

This might be good.

"Some of you will be naturals. Some of you will not be so great. It's okay. Let's just learn, exercise, and have some fun."

As soon as Mrs. Croll gave me the stick, I knew I was in it to win it. I wanted to kill, yoke up, and destroy my opposing team. I did too. I started knocking chicks down left and right. I couldn't have Tony or a spot in the play, but damn it, I'm going to have that fucking puck.

The hockey puck slid my way, and I had a clear shot of the net. I wasn't even far from it- just ten feet away.

Out of nowhere came the biggest chick in my graduating class. When I looked up, the game was over, my body was glued to the floor, and my homegirl Kiesha was standing over me.

"What is wrong with you?" she asked.

"Nothing."

"First you tellin' Mrs. Vega that you basically don't want to play in the stupid musical. Then you're cursin' in gym class about some self-proclaimed love of football that I didn't even know you had until now. Now, you knocking over bitches left and right. So what gives, boo?"

"Nothing." I said a little firmer.

"I noticed that you ain't with 'white bread' no more. That's good. Girl, I was worried that you'd gone off the deep end."

"His name is Tony, and I am so sorry that my taste in people keeps you up at night." I retorted, slightly annoyed.

"Girl, ain't nobody worried over that white dude. I am worried about you though. You've gotten so... so mean."

"I have not."

"Yes, you have. You've changed and not for the better. It's like you are mad at life or something like that."

"You know, you're right. I am mad at life. I am mad at people telling me who I can love. I am mad at people telling me that I am too young to love. I am even angrier at people dictating the things I should be doing. For example, I don't want to play the violin in that God damn play. I want to sing. What about what I want? What about what I need? I mean, we spend all our lives doing things for other people. When we finally have time to do things for ourselves, the opportunity has passed us by. I don't... no, I cannot live my life like that. Fuck that!"

"Chick, you a little too stressed out. Maybe you ought to chill and just worry about what is in front of you right now. I know, let's get blowed."

Imma pretend like I didn't hear that last part. Last thing I need is my momma smelling weed on my clothes. Nope.

"Um, good idea. Let's see what's in front of me right now. Well, I spend all of my time playing this dumb violin. When I am not doing that, I am studying and trying to keep my grade point average up for college, and when I am not doing that, I am watching my siblings, and..."

"And when you're not doing any of those things you are the saddest seventeen year old girl in the room. It's his loss, Jade- not yours.

"His loss, huh? Then why am I crying all the time? Why is it such a chore to go to school? I used to treat school like a job. I would come here to do my work and go home. Now every time I enter this place, it feels like a prison. I feel trapped. I feel like I cannot be happy. I feel..."

"You feel too damn much, and that's the problem. Just have some fun."

"What's fun?" I asked sarcastically.

"Let's go to a movie and then go to the mall this weekend."

"I can't Kiesha, my mom is working, and I have to watch my little brothers."

"Okay so you can't go out with me, but the point is... even though you're sad, find something that you like to do and do it. You like singing, right?"

"Yes. But I don't have any music."

"Well dear, that's a damn lie. You have your violin."

120

"You're right. I do have my violin. I will always have this damn thing!" I laughed.

I guess, I will always have this damn violin whether I want it or not. Fuck my life.

"Then play and sing until all that sadness goes away."

"Okay." I hugged Kiesha so tightly that we both almost passed out. She saved my life and career that day, and I didn't even know it.

27

Believe it or not, March's heartbreak and April's disappointment faded as I took Kiesha's advice. I threw out my sheet music. Okay, so I hid it under my bed. But what followed was something of a miracle. I put on my Sinatra album, and listened. I didn't sing. I didn't play. I just listened.

121

I listened to the chord changes, the crescendos and the decrescendos. I listened to the arias and scales and themes. I listed to the way Frank felt, as if he was singing in front of me and not on a CD. It wasn't just merely classical jazz. It was Frank's life. It was Frank's spirit. It was what I needed to learn to be a real musician and not just a mediocre sheet reader.

I did the same thing for my Aretha Franklin CD. Then I moved onto Billie Holliday. I even listened to Vandross and Babyface. I ended it with Parliament. I spent hours in my room listening out for my siblings and making sure that they did not kill themselves. At the same time, I spent those same hours listening to the souls behind the melodies.

I didn't listen to my insecurities or my frailties. I didn't think about why Tony flip-flopped on me. Hot and cold. Hot and cold. One day he loves me. The next day, I'm old news. I didn't care about not having a chance to sing or play football in the cold spring air. I just existed. I became one with my spirit and my violin.

Then one day, I took my violin and placed it between that special spot between my neck and shoulder blade. I started playing the music and singing- without sheet music or a conductor or a rhythm section. I played, and it wasn't a chore. It was pure bliss, and I was happy.

28

The next day at school, I was the first one in my chair. I didn't even think about Tony. Tony who? Mrs. Vega passed out some new sheet music for our spring festival. It dawned on me that it would be my last spring festival as first chair in high school. Next year, I would be gone- a faded memory on the bland walls and halls of another Chicago Public School building. My aura would disappear from its stale universe.

I chuckled at the thought of leaving this place and all its glory behind. I laughed because I came to this place as a freshman ready to leave it. Now, I had two months left, and I found myself wanting to stay and dragging my feet. But I couldn't. The only thing I could do now is play whatever sheet music Mrs. Vega gave me to the best of my abilities. I was going to do it, too. Play!

I looked at the title. It read Gershwin: *Summertime.* I went over the notes in my head. I knew it came from an opera. *Porgy and Bess*, I think. I remember reading about it in my music theory class. It sounded lame so I didn't even bother renting the movie to watch the opera in its entirety, as my teacher suggested. -I dismissed it. I couldn't fathom how a woman, in her right mind, would want a beggar for a man, and why would she leave him for someone who beats her? She was such a dumbass.

Oh well, the notes on the page didn't sound half bad in my mind's ears.

I took my bow out and lathered it in resin. I shook my bow to get the excess resin off and played the first four bars. Whoa. My mind was blown. I played another four bars... and then another. The music took me to a place that I had never been before. It was the sort of classical music that I had learned how to play over the last four years, but there was something there that the other sonnets and symphonies did not have.

It had jazz. It had sadness. It had beauty. It was maddening. Before long, I was adlibbing to the music. Everyone started sitting down and getting their instruments out, and I continued to play. I didn't care if I hit all the wrong notes because it felt really good to play and be madly in love with what I was playing.

I played the last note, and to my surprise, I heard nothing. It was silent. No one was gossiping or playing their instruments. I looked up, and everyone's eyes were on me. Some were glaring. Some were staring. Some eyes looked like they were summoned up by aliens. I was never so happy to hear Mrs. Vega's shrieking voice break such an uncomfortable silence.

"Now that's how it's supposed to be played, Ms. Jade! All the wonderment of this masterpiece was just told through Ms. Jades strings! I want everyone to play it like that for the spring festival. I want tears coming out of the audience's eyes. Tears, I say!"

I was confused. I was just playing the music for the first time, and now Mrs. Vega was telling everyone to follow my lead. Me, a leader? What weird planet am I on today? My mind wondered. I didn't even know what to say, my body followed the music. My body and spirit blended into my instrument, and I'm supposed to show them my lead? I was so lost in my thoughts and insecurities. I didn't even hear Mrs. Vega screaming my name.

"Jade? Jade? Jade?!"

"Yes, Mrs. Vega?"

"Ms. Jade, please tell us what you did to capture Gershwin?"

Capture Gershwin? Is she fucking serious? I just played what was in my heart- my broken heart.

Don't say that, Jade. It sounds stupid.

"I didn't do anything. I just saw the notes and played them. It's an opera, right? Maybe if we watch it, we can feel how the song is supposed to be played."

Good girl, Jade. Deflect! Let's hope she buys it.

"Great idea," Mrs. Vega shrieked. "Everybody, we're going to watch the opera- not the whole opera, but just enough so you can get the context. I need you guys to be wide awake to play the music the way Jade just played it, and I fear watching a whole opera would be counterproductive to that." Everyone laughed, including myself.

"So everyone take five minutes, warm up, and I will be back with the tape."

Twenty minutes later, Mrs. Vega came back with a boy, a huge TV on wheels, and a DVD in her hand. She appeared determined. Who knew my playing could inspire someone else? To me, my playing was just math on paper-the only math I could stand to deal with. It was the only math I knew. I knew it was art because people told me that it was art in my music theory and my other fine arts classes. Yet, to me, it was just a way out of poverty and sometimes out of my own mind.

Mrs. Vega popped the DVD in the player, turned the lights out, and in no time, we were all quietly watching Gershwin. Normally, when it's dark, we'd take the chance to talk and joke around, but no one was joking now. It was so quiet, we could have heard hay drop. Fuck a pin. We were all staring at the screen watching this short black stout woman singing *Summertime* to a baby.

It's a lullaby, Jade. It's a fucking lullaby. But it's beautiful and sad and… and a hopeful lullaby. It's hopeful.

Maybe I connected with the song because it was so promising and yet sad, but also quite hopeful. Whatever it was made of, it lit a fire in my belly. I wanted to sing those words while I played the song. I wanted to be the short black woman singing it so gracefully. I wanted my violin to be the baby that I was singing the song to. I knew then how I wanted to play it. I knew how I wanted to lead- from the battlefront! If I couldn't sing in the musical, I was going to sing in the festival. But somehow, someway, I was going to sing and play. Play and sing!

Mrs. Vega turned the TV off and told us to get our instruments out. Her fierce eyes were staring at me. Her eyes were asking me what I was going to do. I stood up to her challenge. I started the first four bars with my voice. I sang, "Summertime... and the living is easy..." With my violin, I played the rest, and the orchestra followed adlib and all. They didn't miss a beat or a note either. I looked up after it was over, and mean old Mrs. Vega was crying, "Excellence!"

I finally knew what she wanted from me for the last four years. She wanted me to *feel* the music. She wanted the passion, the sadness, and the burden of the notes to ooze out of my skin like sweat. She wanted me to open my heart and love something other than myself. But I already had loved something or someone other than myself.

Tony taught me that. I was wide open for him whether he cared for me or not. With him, I let myself feel emotions that I thought were never possible. I had no idea it would be a Pandora's Box for other things as well, but I am grateful to him because now I am making art- the stuff that the teachers taught me about in my music theory and my other fine arts class.

The class bell rang, and a few of my friends gave me praises of "dope" and "dats wassup". I packed my violin in its case and started to head out, but Mrs. Vega stopped me.

"Jade, baby girl, come here."

"Yes, Mrs. Vega?" I asked. I knew I wouldn't be able to get away Scott free this time. She knew.

"Ms. Jade, are you okay?"

131

"Yes, I am." I lied, but again, she knew.

"Okay, hunney." She left it at that.

Years later, I knew what she was asking me. She was asking me if I was sad because when musicians play something really well, you can't help but think that they are carrying all of the sadness in the world in their bosom. What we see in their music is only a small piece.

29

When people see you at your most vulnerable, you become less of a threat and more... human. After I played *Summertime*, I opened myself up to my classmates, my school, and the world. I no longer longed to get the notes right. I wanted to *play* them right. My objectives and my viewpoint changed, and so did my social circles.

Classmates that I knew existed for the last four years, but that I had nothing in common with, came up to me. They started talking to me and asking me about my life, my likes, and my dislikes. Dudes were asking me to carry my violin. I found myself "hanging out" and going to the movies after school.

I thought my mom would trip because I was acting different, or I felt different at least. I felt like I was winning. Notifications from my colleges came back, and I was accepted to both schools. I didn't care too much about keeping my grade point average up after learning of my acceptance because fuck that.

I was really feeling myself. The musical went great. The spring festival went great. I was looking forward to going away to college. My life was like my violin playing-absolutely musical. I was on cloud nine of high school success... until I saw Kiesha.

"Girl, wassup, superstar?" Kiesha asked me with her eyes happier and bouncier than usual.

"Whatever, girl. How you doing?" I was laughing at her enthusiasm. It was refreshing, overwhelming, and contagious.

"Girl, I'm good. I'm getting my shit ready for prom. How 'bout you? Who you going to prom with?" She asked.

Damn it, Jade. How could you forget prom? You know, those chicken heads talked about prom every day in history class. How could you forget it? You know what this means?"

"Prom?" I asked nauseously.

"Yes, prom! Oh girl, please don't tell me that you forgot prom? What the hell is the matter with you?"

"I was too busy getting some happy. I forgot. I don't want to go anyway so whatever."

"Look, you gotta go. You don't want to be one of those losers who are like 'I should have gone to prom', do you?"

134

"No, but I am happy. Isn't that what you told me to do- get some happy?

"I told you to forget about that asshole that was making you unhappy and making you lose your damn mind. I didn't say shit about forgetting prom. So what are you going to do?"

"I don't know. I got four weeks. There are at least a hundred boys that go to our school so I am just going to start asking. Shit, I will even pay for my own ticket and shit."

"Chick, is you for real? You are too cute to ask someone. Plus, girls don't ask guys to prom."

"Girl, it's almost the new millennium, and you still on that sexist shit? I'm my own person. I can ask whoever da hell I want."

"Alright, but you're going to look like a mad square asking these lame ass dudes to the prom."

"Yeah, well at least I won't go stag," I retorted.

Ha! You know you're fucked, right? Capital F-U-C-K-E-D!

30

"Hey ma!"

"Yes, Jade?"

"How you feel about me skipping prom? We could save the money for college. You know, prom is too expensive anyways."

"What are you talking about, Jade? You're going to prom."

"But momma, I really don't want to go to prom. I mean, I really really don't want to go to prom."

"Look, you're going to prom, Jade. I'm not letting you miss out on this once in a lifetime experience. You can get married many times, yes, but you only go to prom once."

"Okay, well if I have to go, can I go alone?"

"No."

"Please."

"No!"

"Please, pretty please. I have no one to go with," I begged with everything I had.

"Look, you're pretty. You can find someone to go to prom with. Having a prom date is all a part of the experience."

"So you don't find anything old fashioned about getting dressed up and having a guy come pick you up? C'mon, mom. It's almost the new millennium."

"Look, you're going on your prom. You're getting a dress. You're going with a date. I don't give a fuck if it's old fashioned. I don't give a fuck about the millennium. You're going to prom! End of discussion. And I suggest you find a date soon because if you don't, I'm going to make you take your cousin."

"NO! Mom!"

"End of the fucking discussion, missy. You better get on your grind."

F-U-C-K!!!!!!

31

It was officially May. I was officially on my grind for finding a prom date. I thought about all of the guys I knew who weren't already taken by some other half crazed teenage girl. I wrote their names on a list with the classes that I thought we shared. I heard Nancy Sinatra in my mind ask me, "Are you ready boots? Start walking!" And so I did.

Tony was on the top of my list as my ideal candidate, but seeing how I asked him to take me back several times, I scratched his name off the list three times

138

for good measure. I scratched his name so hard that I made a hole in the paper. Serves him right. Douche.

The next guy on the list was Bill. Bill was a tall guy on the school's basketball team. His body looked like a Venetian God, but his brain resembled a marshmallow. I scratched him off the list purely out of principle.

Then there was Dre. Although I knew Dre from kindergarten, he smoked way too much weed. Dre was a very smart guy, but the weed made him too deep for me. We would talk about cars that we would buy someday, and then he'd go on a tangent about poverty in Somalia within seconds. I didn't want to deal with that shit on prom night, so he was scratched as well.

I then asked Jon, Jimmy, and Todd. They were of proper beauty and intelligence standards for seventeen year old boys. Yet, they all said no. Normally, I would be crushed by such rejection, but they all had the same odd excuse: "Nope. You're Tony's girl".

ME: "No, I am not! We broke up".

THEM: "You're Tony's girl, and we ain't messing with that".

I then asked another twelve guys in futility. They all gave me the same excuse: "Tony's girl".

Damn, Jade. This asshole broke your heart into tiny pieces and has made it impossible for you to get a prom date!

In the words of my favorite South Park character: "You Bastards!" I was my own woman. I thought my own thoughts, and did what I felt- always. Yet, somehow, some way, the things I wanted most were always out of my control. "Well, Tony. You're the fucking gift that keeps on giving. I guess I'm your girl. What a fucking shame that you don't want me," I muttered to myself.

I stormed out of school that day. I left the violin and my textbooks there. It was like the earth opened up and swallowed me whole, but instead of accepting my fate, I foolishly fought. I had to fight. It was my right to fight, damn it! I fought for my right to live my life the way I wanted to live it.

I fought because I was being forced. I was being forced to go to a prom that I didn't want to go to. I was being forced to find a date so that I wouldn't be forced to go with my cousin. I was forced to ask dumbasses and be constantly rejected. I was forced to not go with the asshole that I wanted to go with. And that asshole was forcing me to be rejected by over 15 different guys!

I bet he had a meeting with them in some evil teenage boy lair. I bet they all agreed, "Jade is off limits. Never mind that she is beautiful, sweet, and talented. Just treat her like a leper."

I bet they all agreed in unison to torment me. I bet not one soul objected and said, "This may not be the right thing to do."

"Well fuck them all. Fuck mom, fuck Tony, and fuck the futile 15! Fuck the traditions of prom and the stupid fucking standards that society sets for girls like me. Fuck errrybody. Who da fuck does that ass think he is?" I shouted to the sky.

I was so hot that day that the green grass that bloomed the night before quickly turned brown under my feet. If I wasn't the fire sign of the Leo before, I was that day. I was engulfed in rage. Maybe it was good thing that I left my books and violin at school. They were both made out of wood after all.

32

May 1998 taught me a life's lesson: time flies when you're under a scathing deadline with a side of impending doom. My happy heart sunk into a deep depression as I realized that I would be taking my cousin, Sam, to the prom. I found it so ironic that my mom was willing to make my prom night the most horrible night of my life just so that I could attend this once in a lifetime experience. I found that notion so hilariously ironic that I started laughing violently while walking to my class. I spilled into the hallway with laughter.

Momma is protecting me. I laughed.

Momma wants me to have fun taking my cousin to a prom where all my friends would know that I did not have a date. I laughed harder.

I laughed so hard that I didn't see the Greek tragedy that stood in front of me. I didn't see Tony. I avoided him for the last few weeks. I didn't want to tear up anymore if I could help it. Tony's rejection was the worst because he was actually someone I cared about. Yet, there he stood: six feet, brown hair, and blue eyes wrapped up it my rejection. If one could look closely at his shoes, they would notice the small specks of blood where he stepped on my heart and turned it to mush. This day was turning out to be a winner indeed.

"Jade?"

"Yes, Tony." I said as coldly as possible.

That's right! Be cool. No, be cruel.

"Jade?"

"That is my name, Tony. What do you want?" Again, as cold as I could be.

"Can we talk?" He looked nervous.

"No. I have to go."

Yes, girl. Be cruel.

"Can we talk later?" He persisted.

"We can talk never!"

That's a good one- an oldie but a goodie. But awfully childish. He looks sad. He's cute when he looks sad. He's cute all of the time.

Never mind that shit. Fuck Tony.

"Don't be silly. Talk to me for a second."

"About what?"

"About prom and you going with me." His blue eyes got bigger and bluer. I didn't think it was possible for his eyes to get bluer. His pink lips turned into a smirk.

Is this dude serious? Does he honestly think I would go with him after he rejected me all of those times?

Say no, Jade.

"What about prom?" I snapped.

"Do you have anyone to go with?"

C'mon girl, he knows the answer to this. Him and the futile 15 know the fucking answer to this.

"Just my cousin." He laughed. I glared. "No seriously, just my cousin because for some reason all of the guys I asked turned me down." I glared again with an eyebrow raised.

"Really?" He asked sheepishly.

Wow, what a complete ass. He knew what he did!

"Yes. By the way, did you have anything to do with that?" I asked.

"Nope." He lied.

He's a GODDAMN liar, Jade! Run away!

"Well, do you want to go with me?" He deflected.

"No."

"C'mon, Jade."

Like a Phoenix emerging from the sun, his beautiful brown hair lit me on fire me as it glistened under the hall lights. His beauty enraged me so much that it took me back to all of those days that I asked for his hand as my date. It

146

took me back to all of those days that he turned me down. Before I knew it, I was shouting at him.

"Look, you broke up with me. You told the guys to turn me down. I know you did that much. Then when I asked you, you rejected me... not once, but like six times. So why should I go with you?"

"You asked me," he said.

"What?" I said puzzled by his reaction.

"You asked me." He firmly repeated.

"Huh?" I just wasn't getting him.

"Look, Jade. I'm old fashioned. I like to be the one asking the girl."

"That's stupid."

"That's me."

"Well, you're stupid! Look, I make my own destiny. I don't have time to wait for someone to ask me. If I want something, I go after it with all the ferocity that I can

muster. I suggest you do the same."

"With ferocity, huh?"

"Yes, you jerk. I don't play games. I know what I

want. I assess the situation. Then, I reach my objective."

"Love is not an objective, Jade."

"Everything is an objective, Tony. Even if love is

not an objective, at least I have the good sense not to let

what I truly want pass me by. I said no! I would rather go

with my cousin!"

Good girl! Stand up for yourself.

It might have been one of the few and rare

occasions that Tony took my advice because he didn't let

me leave. I started to walk away, and he grabbed me by

waist. He pulled me close to his chest. I felt his heart beat

through our shirts. He tilted my chin upwards, and then he

kissed me.

My mind was no longer saying, "Tony, who?"

My mind was saying, "Again, Tony."

His kiss felt like I was wrapped in a current of warm water. His pink lips put my raging fire out for the first time in months. I remembered what his arms felt like when they were wrapped around me at the pier and when they stopped me from falling on the ground. His arms felt safe. I was safe. I was not safe. I was under his spell again.

I felt my mind scream: "flee!" I felt my heart shout: "more!" I was confused. For the first time in my life, my objective was not clear. At the same time, my heart was clear as a day of unrestricted visibility on an ocean front horizon. I knew that I only wanted Tony. But did he want me?

Looking back on those days I had no idea of his intentions. I knew he rejected me, tormented me, and laid in my nightmares waiting to tell me that he did not want

149

me or that he did not love me. But this time, his arms told me a different story. They told me that he longed to hold me and only me. He didn't let me go, and I felt his aura imprint on mine. His arms told me that he loved me when his lips were silent or simply spouting bullshit, which was most of the time.

I was paralyzed with love, lust, joy, excitement, enchantment, and enlightenment. Hell, you name it. I had it. But all I could actually say was: "Yes, Tony."

33

It's funny how a kiss can change your world from impending doom to an eternal heaven. I was on cloud nine courtesy of Tony Georgino. I almost started living up to my last name, Valentine. I couldn't get enough of him. For the next few weeks, we were inseparable. He was the air, and I was the flame that danced in it. I thought I hated him, especially after what he put me through over the past few months. But it seemed as if my hate evaporated or burned itself alive. Soon, nothing else mattered but him.

Tony and I went everywhere. The city was our playground, and we acted our age. We were so young and so in love or so in lust. I knew which one I was in. Yet, Tony was in love …I think. I started imagining his body in less than holy ways.

I remembered how he embraced me when he asked me to prom a few weeks ago. I remember how warm his body was. I found myself thinking about other parts of his body. I wanted to kiss his face. But I also wanted to kiss his eyebrows, his arms, his chest, his back, and his other parts below.

I wanted to know what made him weak in his knees. I wanted to bite all over him. I just wanted to find out the hard way. I wanted to taste him, and so I did.

One random day, after class was over, I walked right up to Tony. My palms were sweaty, and I had no idea how to be sexy. I just knew that I needed to be sexy. I wanted Tony. I wanted him like I wanted an Easy Bake Oven as a child. I didn't care if I had to sell a part of my soul to get him either. I intended to get what I wanted, and my intentions were not pure.

"Tony?" I asked. He turned around.

"Hey, wassup, babe?" He asked. I just grabbed him, and I kissed him. I found myself whispering in his ear: "I want you, now."

"Huh?" He looked extremely surprised and puzzled.

"I love you, and I want you," I said, raising my eyebrow.

"Oh!" He sounded surprised.

Why is he surprised?

152

"Aren't you a virgin?" he asked.

"No. You?" I asked.

"No." He stammered.

He thought you were a virgin, Jade. Ha, that is so funny.

"Good. Then we can have each other without worrying about taking one's purity," I laughed.

Look, Jade, he's not laughing.

"That's not funny, Jade. This is serious."

"I know. I know that I seriously want you. I told you that when I want something or someone, I go after it or him or her. Whatever."

"Yes, you do." He laughed. "So when do you want to do this?"

"Now, so we can avoid the cliché of prom, and because I can't wait," I said jumping up and down.

I really can't wait. Please don't make me wait,

Tony.

"Now?" He asked nervously.

"Yes. Or do you not want me?" I started pouting.

"No, we can do it now. I'm just wondering why so suddenly?"

"Oh, Tony! I've wanted you for a long time," I said rather bluntly.

"You have?" He asked nervously.

Jade, look who isn't so sure of himself now. Ha.

"Tony, you're gonna do me now, or you won't get to do me at all." I snapped.

"You know, Jade, you can be very persuasive," he chuckled.

Tony drove us to a really dingy looking motel that afternoon. I didn't care that it was dingy. It could have been a box for all I cared. I just could not wait to get naked

154

in front of him. Although I lost my virginity a year ago, Tony made me feel like it was my first time. I wish he was my first time, too.

I gave my virginity to an ex-boyfriend who I hated at the time that I gave it to him. I don't even remember his name. We were arguing, and I just dished it out like a candy bar to subdue a crying child. I broke up with the asshole a week later. I just wanted to get my virginity out of the way before I went to college. I didn't want to be the new kid on the block with the big V. But with Tony, I wished that I wasn't so goal oriented. I wished the big V wasn't an objective. I wished that Tony was my first.

Tony took off his t-shirt and jeans. His skin was so creamy. The winter months had turned his brown skin to the color of a peach. His arms and chest were fuzzy like a peach, too. The hair on his head was brown, but the ones where no one could see were blonde. I would have never guessed. But I was extremely glad to see all of them.

I raced to take off my clothes. I threw my bra and jeans on the dilapidated armchair in the cheap motel room. I was so eager to feel his body on mine, but I really wanted him *in* me. I wanted our bodies to become one. I wanted him to feel my love as I felt his when I was wrapped in his arms.

I could hear my mother's voice telling me not to cast my pearls before swine. But Tony was no swine. He was my exception. He was my lover. He was mine.

I watched our shadows play on the walls as we played between the sheets, on the bed, on the floor, on the chair, and everywhere else. I watched all the love I had in my heart flow down deep below. My back was cold, but Tony kept me warm with his arms and everything else. He felt hot. I burned as I watched him touch my thighs and kiss my breast and the small of my back.

I relished in taking my turn. I grabbed him, and he winced. I was forceful. I was playful. I was myself. I was happy with him. He looked happy. His eyes moaned while I took my place on top. He was putty in my hands. I was his bronze goddess. He was my reason for living. He was my violin, and I took command of his bow.

My fire sign burned bright, and after two hours of bliss, I laid in his arms. I was so grateful to him and for him. I was grateful to him because he allowed me to be myself. I was grateful to him because he honored my request. I was grateful for him because God sent him to me. I was in love and experiencing love for the first time.

"Tony?" I asked peacefully.

"Yes?" He asked.

"I love you." I told him.

I'll love him forever.

"I love you, too." He told me.

My heart burned so brightly that I thought I was going to die. I felt that he might have been prompted or provoked to say his "I love you" because he was trapped and lying between the softest parts of my thighs. For a fleeting second, I thought that maybe he felt pressured into it, but something told me that he meant this particular "I love you". His eyes and his body confirmed his "I love you".

His eyes, especially, told me the truth. Later on, I found out this particular truth serum the hard way. Tony would lie to me on the phone, via email, and via text. But Tony's eyes never lied to me- not once. They were the windows to his soul. They were always open, and I always walked right through them.

His lips didn't lie to me today, and I was grateful that they were in sync with his eyes. Tony didn't know what he was talking about when he said that soul mates weren't real because if I didn't believe in soul mates before, I met mine that day. For the next few weeks up until prom, all of Chicago was our bedroom; there was nothing cliché about it.

34

I never believed in fairy tales as a girl. I actually thought they were quite scary growing up. The idea of a woman making a slave out of a child, or another woman hunting down a different child because the child was too pretty, was absolutely preposterous to lead to a happy ending- as if those girls would forget all of the trauma and hard times that they had endured once their lips touched their man's lips. It was laughable at best.

159

I also didn't believe in magic. For someone who believes in the power of will and love, I was extremely logical. Everything to me was black and white. No pun intended. Although I was a musician, I was a scientist at heart. I knew that matter could never be destroyed nor created. It just transformed from something else to something better or to something worse. However, prom proved my belief system wrong.

Tony and I- along with the whole senior class- got out of school early to prepare for the magic that was supposed to be prom night. I took advantage of the opportunity by pressing his lips with mine, but all things come to an end. I had to get home. I didn't want to leave Tony's side as we parted ways.

However, my mother demanded that I get home early enough for her to do my hair, my eyebrows, my toes, and whatever medieval torture she had planned for my

160

prom night. I was pretty naturally, but I hated *getting* pretty. Getting pretty sucked. Later in life, I learned that getting pretty was very necessary in life with an almost magical after effect.

Yet, youth led me to believe that the concept of women putting on pounds of make-up to appear naturally prettier seemed stupid and superfluous. Now that I am in my thirties, it still seems stupid and superfluous, sometimes. I've always said if you got it, use it. Don't hide it, especially under tons of make-up. Yet, how does that saying go?: "If you can't beat them, join them." And I joined them that day.

My mother's friend, Nancy, damn near burned my ear off with the black flat iron of death to get my edges straight while my momma whipped up a fifteen-minute pedicure. Like two linebackers at the line of scrimmage, my mother and her friend sacked me. Their weapon of

161

choice: tweezers. After arching my eyebrows and wiping the tears from my eyes, my mother said, "Okay, we're done for now."

Holy Shit, Batman, that hurt. They're done for now? This is a football game that I don't wanna play.

Although my mother's words frightened me, nothing scared me more than Tony picking me up. He was my man, and I was his girl. Yet, I still felt that I wasn't pretty enough or that I wasn't ever going to be pretty enough or, maybe, he would find out how hideous I really was. Nothing could have been further from the truth, but you could not have told my racing heart that I was good enough.

After the torture was done, my mother became an extra on *Speed Racer* as she drove me from Nancy's apartment to ours. She marched me up the stairs and dunked me in perfume. I think it was Elizabeth Taylor's

162

White Diamonds. I didn't like it too much, but I guess it was glamorous. It did have a sparkly top. Yet, I was more of a soap and water and deodorant kind of girl.

"Hurry up. You're late." My mom was screaming at me.

"Mom, he's on his way. I'm already an hour late. I don't think waiting five minutes for me to put on my dress will matter," I stalled.

"If you get there too late and miss your photos, girl, I will buss you upside your head!"

"Mom. Please stop trippin!" It was bad enough that my heart was bulging from my chest. I just couldn't take her screaming at me or any other excitement.

"I ain't playing!"

"Yes, momma."

Stockings? Check. Dress? Check. Little brother screaming that Tony's here? Check.

Oh my God! He's here! I really hope he thinks I'm pretty.

Lame-O? Check. Girl, quit trippin. He better be glad you said yes to him.

And take my cousin? Hell No!!

I walked outside and everyone's eyes were on me. Even people walking by stopped dead in their tracks. I was Tyra Banks' fierce, but all I could see was him. All Tony could see was me. We connected twenty feet away. The world was swimming, but time was magical- not logical. Who knew?

My prince stood with me as we took ghetto prom pictures in front of my home. My family, along with other neighborhood kids, posed with the King and Queen. Time was suspended. Time was air, and I was walking on it. Tony placed me in his whip like I was fine China on a glass shelf.

He wasn't so bad himself. He was actually kind of dashing with a side of dorky but absolutely perfect.

No. Tony was simply dashing. I didn't even want to go to prom. I got what I wanted- seeing my handsome man in a tuxedo. I just wanted to lie in his arms and kiss his forehead and whatever else my lips could find. But momma wanted pictures, and momma gets what momma wants.

"We're late, Jade, really late." He said.

"So?"

"So, we're probably going to miss everything."

"So?"

"Aren't you upset?" He shouted.

"Nope. As long as I get pictures and as long as I am with you, I don't care what we do."

"You don't?" He looked surprised by my nonchalance.

"Nope. I actually don't even want to go to prom."

"Well, what do you want to do?" Tony asked sheepishly.

I tugged at his belt, and bit my lip. I was trying so hard not to jump his bones as he drove away. Tony was so fucking sexy- dorky but sexy. Tony was my drug and seeing him in his tux was especially intoxicating. My heart was going to burst. I didn't think there was a better way of leaving this earth.

"You're insatiable, Jade."

"You like it though," I flirted.

"Yeah, you're probably right."

I didn't think Tony and I looked fabulous as a couple at first. We didn't even know what each other was wearing, but somehow we managed to complement each other. My dress was a teal green that complimented my olive complexion. I had the dress tailored so that it could outline my every curve- curves that Tony knew too well.

Tony's suit was black with a teal bow and vest. He didn't know the color of my dress, and it was almost serendipitous that we matched. I never had the chance to tell him because I found my dress one week before prom at the bottom of the clearance bin. But I cleaned up nicely. We both cleaned up nicely, together.

Moreover, growing up on the Westside of Chicago, it was an annual event for people to look at the prom goers and make a big fuss. Thus, I didn't think anything of it when neighbors stopped and stared at Tony and me. Nonetheless, prom itself was a whole new story.

When Tony and I walked into the Hilton, our friends didn't recognize us. We were like real royalty. Classmates stopped and stared. Only my BFF knew who the real Cinderella was.

"Jade!" Kiesha screamed.

"Hey girl!" I shouted back.

"Damn, girl. You look hot, huh? Whitebread don't look too bad himself."

"Kiesha, his name is Tony! You are so disrespectful!"

"Girl, whatever, at least he ain't your cousin," she laughed.

"Girl, don't even play. My momma was serious as a heart attack," I laughed back.

"Chick, take your pictures. You know your momma don't play."

"I'm already on it. Tony, are you ready?" I turned around and motioned to Tony that it was picture time. He followed me like a lost pup.

You must look really awesome, Jade. Tony is usually not this quiet or submissive.

Yup!

Tony and I took our pictures. We posed like we were extras on the *Young and Restless.* At least that's what my godmother said once she saw the prom pictures. My godmother declared Tony a wolf and ordered me to ditch him. I told her that I loved him. She said that she didn't like him.

Cinderella's godmother never told Cinderella to ditch the prince. But my godmother didn't call Tony a prince. She called him a wolf.

But Tony was my prince, and that picture didn't count. The photo made us look too passionate, too grown, and too sexy. It didn't reflect the real love that we felt for one another or at least the love that I felt for him.

The picture didn't reflect Tony showing me how to dance in an empty baseball field when he found out that I didn't know how to waltz as the sun set below the earth.

169

The picture didn't reflect the warmth that I felt every time he held me in his arms. It didn't reflect us holding each other as we waited for the traffic jam in the parking lot to clear after our prom was over. It didn't reflect the moment that fireworks lit the sky like diamonds when we kissed. Diamonds are forever. Pictures are not.

35

Whatever high that May bestowed upon me was robbed by June. June delivered two devastating blows. The first was that my mother didn't complete my FAFSA form, which meant I had to go to the cheaper of the two schools. The second blow was that the cheaper school was far from Tony.

Graduation was no longer a rite of passage or a goal I wanted to achieve. Graduation signified death-death of the new love that I wanted so desperately to keep. As such, the once small and dismal light at the end of

170

tunnel became a blaring migraine burning brightly. The graduation train was coming and its echoing horn raised a familiar horror in my heart.

Tony didn't seem fazed. He was always so linear and so logical. I could see him calculating what to do with our relationship as he held my hand and carried my books for the last time. It was as if I was waiting for the relationship guillotine. Walking through the halls even while holding his hand was like walking the row. I could have sworn I heard someone say, "dead teenage love affair walking". Our love was on the chopping block, but I wasn't ready to give it up yet.

I often asked Tony if he loved me. He always answered "Yes" or "Yup". But he never said it, except that one time he was trapped between the softness of my curves. I know now that maybe he couldn't bring himself to say it to my face sober without the highs of sex. Maybe

171

if he said "I love you," it would make our love real and not

some young stupid thing he did when he was kid. Saying

those words would make me hard to forget, and he had to

forget me. I was an obstacle to his success. He was an

obstacle to mine. Everyone knew it. Everyone said it. I

didn't want to believe it. It was something that I refused to

believe. It was something that I fought until the very end.

On graduation day, I was excited and sad. I was

excited because I was going to introduce Tony to my dad

for the first time. My momma didn't care for Tony. She

thought he was too brazen for his age. That's what I loved

about him. I knew my dad would love him, too.

My momma and dad had gotten divorced when I

was three. I think they only agreed on two things. The first

thing they agreed on was that they loved me. The second

thing they agreed on was that they loved *Star Trek: The*

Next Generation. I never thought that they could agree on another thing. But this year, I watched miracles happen.

After the graduation ceremony was over, I stole Tony away from his parents. We marched right up to my stepmother and dad. My whole body was grinning with excitement. I pushed Tony in front of my dad and gave him an introduction worthy of British royalty.

"Dad, this is Tony. He's extremely smart and funny, and he's also my boyfriend."

"Tony, this is my dad."

They both held out their hands and shook them. I thought: Success! I thought wrong. My dad smiled. Tony smiled. Tony left and told me that he would call me soon. My dad pulled me aside "mafia sit down" style. I was not prepared for what my dad said next.

"Get rid of him!"

"What?!" I asked. No, I demanded to know why my dad, who only exchange two sentences with my beloved, wanted me to get rid of the love my life.

"I said get rid of him?!"

"But, why, daddy?"

"I don't like the way he shook my hand. It felt weird. You can tell a lot about a man from his handshake. Also, I just don't like him."

I felt all the anger of a caged lion. I felt hopeless. I felt mad. I was volatile. I was feverish. I was fury. I felt myself wanting to say words that I never had the guts to say. This time was different. This time I said them.

"Daddy, I love him!" I shouted. *Oh my god, Jade. You're shouting at your dad. Have you gone batshit crazy?*

I yelled at my dad, but he didn't move or flinch. He looked amused. His amusement made me angrier.

174

"Didn't you hear what I said? Daddy, I love him." I announced again as if he didn't hear me the first time.

"Baby, sweetie, hunney. You're going away to school. You're going to be famous someday. You won't have time for him. Plus, guys like him are a dime a dozen. You're too young to know what love means anyway. What are you, sixteen?"

"Daddy, I'm seventeen, and I love him!"

"Sixteen. Seventeen. Six of twelve. Half a dozen. It doesn't matter. In a year, you'll be saying, 'Tony, who?'"

"No I won't, dad. He's different. He's special."

"Tony, who?!" My dad reiterated. I dropped the conversation knowing that it would lay on deaf ears.

I watched my dad walk away, and I hurried back to my mother's side. My mascara was running, and my momma saw the tears run down my cheek.

175

"What's the matter, baby?" my momma tenderly inquired.

"Daddy says Tony and I won't last. Daddy says next year I'll be saying, 'Tony, who?' I was fighting back the tears while explaining what my father said and failed completely.

"Well, sweetie, your daddy is right. But it's okay. Men for you will be a dime a dozen." My momma tried to comfort me, but failed miserably.

I was in complete awe. My mother and father couldn't agree on anything before my graduation. They hadn't agreed on anything since my graduation. But they agreed that Tony would be gone by my second year of college. It's a shame when the only thing that your parents can agree on is your impending failure at love. June wasn't even halfway over, and I was TKO-ed three times.

Yet, fuck all that. I loved Tony. I was going to fight for our love. I didn't care what it cost me. I was going to keep him in my heart for as long as I could breathe. I was going to do the impossible. Tony would stay Tony. He would not become "Tony who?" Why? Because I was not going to give up! I was not going to stop fighting. I was not going to stop loving. No matter what happened, I would be true to my heart. I would stay true to myself.

36

June sucker punched me hard. If I was made of a smarter composition, I would have dumped Tony and cut my losses. But I was a fool in love. So I did the exact opposite. I loved him harder for the next two months. I loved him harder than anyone could love another human being. I loved him harder than anyone I subsequently loved for that matter.

I called Tony almost every day. There wasn't any shame in my game. If I only had two months to spend with him, I was going to spend as many days as I could wrapped in his love. I kissed him all over the school, the park, the movies, and the rest of Chicago. I also kissed him all over his body and other places that a lady shouldn't mention. I don't think there was an inch of his body that I left untouched. There was not an inch of me that he didn't kiss as well. My daddy always said that I left no rock unturned. I turned over all of Tony's rocks.

People disapprovingly shook their heads as we walked by draped in our love. I saw them. I always wondered if Tony saw their disapproving stares. Although the sun turned Tony's skin brown, he was still white. Although my skin was fair, my hair was nappy and my ass was big. I didn't look black, but I looked "other."

People would stop and look at him and then at me. They would look at me a little longer as if fifteen additional seconds would give them my D.N.A. codes. I swear. Chicago could be so wonderful and yet so racist at times. But fuck that. I had Tony. I was invincible.

When I wasn't with Tony, I was at home with my violin playing the great jazz standards. I copped another Frank Sinatra album with a better rendition of *The Summer Wind*. I took out my violin and hummed the words as my bow glided over the strings. Normally, playing my violin was my greatest joy- second to Tony's lips, his arms, and his everything else. But this time, the words – not the notes- struck me like a double edged sword. They cut me hard. I was betrayed by my true love. I was betrayed by my savior. I was betrayed by my music.

I finally got what ole Frankie Blue Eyes' song meant. Growing up, I thought it was a jazzy tune, but it was real life. It was my future. I imagined that Tony and I were a summer wind and then when winter would come, we would disappear along with our love. I lowered my bow and then my head. I opened the CD player. I took out the CD and chucked it across the room. Mr. Sinatra wasn't going to ruin my day today. I stuck in Etta James and started playing *At Last.*

July rolled into August. August meant a new school and a new life. College also meant no Tony. I wasn't ready for August, but Tony was very helpful, especially the day before I left. Tony must have sensed my despair or viewed his calendar because he called me. He also picked me up within thirty minutes of his phone call.

I loved our conversations. I loved being in his presence. I even loved when we fought because we would make up soon after. More than anything, I was really addicted to his arms. I could live my whole life in his hugs.

He could ask me to marry him with a hug instead of a ring, and it would have been all that I needed.

As much as I loved Tony's hugs, I wanted his entire body that day. I wanted to curl up inside it. I wanted to ride on top of it. I wanted to take a mental picture- no, a mental sculpture- of his body. I needed to because it would be four months before I would see him again. Four months is such a long time, especially when you're seventeen.

Tony must have sensed how I felt because he was pulling his dad's truck in front of a motel on the southwest side. The motel seemed even dingier than the ones we had been to before. Yet, I didn't care. Even if it was a cardboard box, I was going to take him one way or another.

"Whadya say, Jade?" Tony smirked. He knew what I wanted. I was dirtier and edgier than him. I think that's

181

why he loved me so much. I was everything he wasn't. The feeling was more than mutual.

"You know what I want," I said.

We ran to our room upstairs, and I immediately started pulling his clothes off. He was wearing a tacky Hawaiian shirt. Under it, he was wearing a white tank top. I was more interested in what laid underneath his tank. Even though it was summer, his chest was a pale pink. But his arms were a tan brown. Both his arms and chest were hard and mesmerizing. I started with his shirt. I didn't have time for his buttons. My bus was leaving the next day, and my time was short.

"Whoa, I need to wear that shirt back home. My parents are going to trip if I show up naked." He joked.

"They will? I won't." I teased and laughed.

"Jade, this is serious. Quit acting like a child."

"I'm not acting like a child. I am simply stating that I like seeing you naked," I smirked.

"Naked?"

"Yes, and please hurry. I don't have time to wait all damn day!" I commanded.

"Yes, ma'am!" Tony obliged.

"Tony, you don't like this shirt, do you?" I asked holding his ugly Hawaiian shirt in the air.

"Well, yes. It's my favorite shirt. Why'd you ask?"

"Well, you wear it a lot. I think it's ugly, but it has your scent. I want to keep it at school for when I miss you."

"That's stupid, Jade." He teased.

"You're stupid, Tony. No. For real. I want to keep it. It will remind me of you when I miss you cause you know I will miss you terribly." I was glancing between his deep blue eyes and his shirt.

"You know, I don't even have a scent." He protested.

"Yes you do. Everyone has a scent. You smell like that shampoo on that commercial. You know the one that the ladies wear?"

"Herbal Essences?"

"Yeah, that one. The fruity smelling one." I laughed. He laughed. We laughed.

"Stop laughing at me," I pleaded. "You know, every time I smell that shampoo, I think you're near me. It's not fair. So give me the damn shirt! That way I won't be tricked so much."

"You make a valid point. Oh well, it's not every day I get to go home naked. Thanks, Jade."

"You're most welcome, Tony. Now, take those damn pants off. I want something else," I demanded.

"Yes, boss!"

184

I wrapped my legs around Tony. I was a ball of energy that day, but something forced me to slow down. I didn't want to move. I wanted to let him take the lead. I wanted to see what he would do with my body if I let him have total control, and he did not disappoint.

He grabbed my hips and rocked me back and forth. My eyes rolled into the back of my head. No. My head cocked back, and I looked up at a pleasant surprise. The dingy motel had a mirror on the ceiling, and I was able to watch the show and participate in it as well.

I didn't see shadows on the walls like all the times before. I saw us in 3D. I saw our bodies become one. I saw him love on every square inch of my body. His soul imprinted on each one of my pores. I saw beads of sweat come off his shoulders and his forehead. His eyes were the bluest I had ever seen them. I was hypnotized. I wondered how I could go on living without him- without looking at his beautiful eyes. For the first time in my life, I wasn't looking for an out. I was looking for an in.

Tony had my lips, my body, my heart, and my pearls. I casted everything I owned to him. I wanted him more as I watched his body move up and down with mine in perfect synchronicity. The sex was great, but it wasn't just sex. I felt like his soul ravaged mine. I was his forever until the end of the earth whether he liked it or not. Whether I wanted to be his or not, I was his.

Tony dropped me off at home. We were silent. We knew of the dawn that we faced- the one where we would not be in each other's presence. We kissed. He held me close, but I didn't want to leave his side. He was my man, but I had a new journey to undertake. I had a new life to make for myself. The next day, I left Chicago and everything in it, including my heart.

37

Although Tony was my heart and I was afraid of losing my heart, he was the least of my worries. On top of going to the cheaper school far away from him and my world, I found out that such cheaper school did not have an orchestra. What that really meant was that I had no opportunity to get any scholarships whatsoever. Four years of Mrs. Vega's "Excellence!" went down a fucking drain.

Oh well, such as life.

Combine that with the fact that my expected family contribution or ("E-F-fucking-C") was five grand a semester, which led me to the real meaning of working for my education. So I found myself without a reason to play my violin, 15 class units, and three fucking minimum wage jobs. If I had any good sense, I would have dropped out of college, went back home to Chicago, and become a street

187

performer. Alas, I had too much pride to practice my craft

for free. After all, I was a trained professional courtesy of

Chicago Public Schools.

My pride led me to work for a book store, a

clothing store, and the dish room in my dorm's cafeteria. It

was probably a blessing that Tony was not there. I had no

time for him. I had no time for sleep! I slept between

classes in the halls of the English, Math, and Science

departments. Wherever there was a student lounge, I was

knocked out. Homework? Forget about it. I was usually an

A student in high school. Yet, in college, I found myself

chanting a new mantra: "C's get degrees!"

I was killing myself to stay in a school that I didn't

want to be at because I had too much pride to come back

to the Chi. Looking back, my life would have been simpler

if I had just gone back. But I was always up for a good

challenge, and this school was kicking my ass.

Being overworked, underpaid, and undereducated had a terrible effect on my spirit. I didn't have Tony to bounce me back. I didn't even have friends to snap me out of it. I went from being a big fish in a small pond to a guppy in the middle of a shark-infested ocean. I had no friends. I had no time for friends. Plus, I couldn't relate to anyone there.

I was a brown needle in a white haystack. I found myself being the only black person around for miles, let alone in my class. I didn't mind white people. Tony's white. All my friends were of diverse backgrounds. But this was a different kind of white. This white came from rich parents and small towns and cornfields. Yet, my auntie told me to stay out of the fucking corn. This white liked Wheezer and Third Eye Blind and Garth Brooks. I couldn't relate to this white being a city girl with classical, jazz, and hip hop tendencies, and I found myself alone and sad.

Yet, Kiesha's words rang in the back of my mind. I could hear her saying, "Girl, get you some happy." So I did. Just because an orchestra did not exist at my university did not mean that I could not make my own. So I did. I was an orchestra of one.

I found myself on the quad with my violin in one hand and my bow in the other playing jazz. For the next three months, I played every Tuesday- the only day I didn't have to rush off to work. I played until my heart couldn't play anymore. I didn't have to worry about having calluses on my hand because Tony was not there to hold it. As a matter of fact, Tony was never where he said he would be. He especially wasn't at home when I called. But that is neither here nor there.

Tony's mom and I were cordial in high school, but that relationship soon became frayed in college. It was mostly my fault. I'd call Tony's home, and she'd always answer. Tony was never there. Looking back, maybe she

wanted to tell me to move on, but she didn't. Tony turned

me into that annoying girl who called way too much. My

heart sank into a deeper depression when I could not hear

his voice.

Girl, don't let this ass do this to you, AGAIN! Find

you some happy.

Ok.

One Friday night in November, I found myself at

the school's open mic. I had never played by myself on a

stage before so I thought that I would give it a try. I found

myself playing that old familiar *Porgy and Bess* tune,

Summertime. I even started it off singing it like I did before.

The crowd of ten people went wild. Before I knew

it, I had played four more songs. I played and adlibbed

mostly to the songs that I performed in high school. But

the audience didn't know that they were high school

songs. To them, I was just some black chick playing a violin, which was odd in itself to people who have never met black people before attending college. They clapped and yelled for more. I played for my new fans and found me some happy.

After the open mic session ended, several people came up to talk to me. They wanted to know how I played so well. They were completely baffled when I told them that I had only played for four years. They thought I was a child protégé or something like that. They were again surprised when I told them that I was a C student- hopefully- and working three jobs to pay tuition. They thanked me again and left. Then the devil walked up to me.

This devil went by the name of Eduardo. He had long jet black hair- the kind that you wanted to play in all day with combs and elaborate brushes. His eyes were stone black and his accent was extremely thick. He walked up to me and told me that he "wiked the dway dat I played."

"Huh?" I had no idea what he had just said. Eduardo cleared his throat and tried a little harder at the King's English.

"I like the way you play," he said clearer than before.

"Oh, thanks," I blushed. He was fine, and I couldn't believe that I was thinking that anyone other than Tony was fine. *This must be what your parents meant when they said, "A dime a dozen."*

"You play with such intensity and passion. You should play for me sometime," he said.

Is this guy serious? Play for him? Bitch, please. I'm not the hired help.

Wait a damn minute, Jade. See if he has a gig for you. Gig spells dollars.

I don't think this cat means "a gig."

Just see.

"What do you mean, play? Like in a gig?" I inquired.

"Si. I spin at the Blue Flash. It's a club downtown. I would love to have you play on top of my records."

"Okay, that sounds great!" I exclaimed in relief.

"What's your name?" he asked.

"Jade. Jade Valentine," I said confidently.

"Jade is a good name. It's a passionate color and strong jewel as well. My name is Eduardo. You can call me Ed if you like, and I hope you like," he flirted. I blushed.

"Um, I rather call you by Eduardo if you don't mind," I stated in my professional voice.

"Sweetheart, you can call me anything you want. Just play your violin for me."

"Thanks, but I'll call you Eduardo. How do I contact you? Do you have an email or phone number?" I asked.

Just then he handed me a piece of paper with his name, phone, and email already filled out. Ed had game, and I could smell it a mile away. I had a split second where I thought I could have made a run for it, but fuck it. I really needed the money. I took Ed's flimsy piece of paper and sealed my fate. Good or bad, I sealed it.

I packed up my violin and went home to my dorm room. I picked up the phone and called Tony. This time he answered. Why didn't he answer before I went to the open mic session? Why didn't he answer before I met Ed?

38

Next week, I found myself calling Ed. I didn't want to, but I needed cash. My class counselor called me into

195

her office, and told me that my midterm grades were not up to par and that I was being placed on "academic probation". I informed her that I was working three jobs to pay tuition.

Although she was extremely nice, her advice was harsh. She basically told me to figure it out because paying tuition would be a moot point if I flunked out of school. So I quit two of my jobs. I kept the cafeteria job because it was in my dorm, which meant that I could get more sleep. It also meant that I had less money and more time to miss Tony. So I called Ed.

Ed told me that he was spinning at the Blue Flash. He told me to come and try it out. I didn't like the way that sounded because it meant that I would be playing for free. Fuck free. I needed loot. When I asked Ed about payment, he informed me that if the crowd liked me, he would consider giving me a permanent segment.

At first, I was pissed. But my anger quickly transformed into gratitude because it meant that I would be playing my violin, and it meant that my name would possibly get out. I could already see my name on the marquee in my mind's eye. I wanted to play, and Ed gave me that opportunity. I wasn't going to fuck it up because of payment issues. I was going to go forth bravely and throw the chips up in the air. Let them land wherever the fuck they may.

Because it was my first time playing at the Blue Flash, Ed invited me over early for a sound check. Because I was playing at a club, I decided to dress a little sexier than normal. It was a cold November day in Central Illinois, so my options were limited. I opted for heels, red leather pants, and a black tank. I looked like a hot biker chick. I laughed at the idea of riding off on a motorcycle with my violin strapped to my back.

I arrived at the Blue Flash around seven. Ed did a sound check, and then he started to spin. I had never heard a deejay spin like Ed. He played all the classics. He was hot like a Latino Tom Cruise. His thick accent made him even hotter. I started to feel faint from his hotness and from starvation, and he noticed.

"Are you okay? You look a little lightheaded."

"It's probably because I forgot to eat."

"Well, let me feed you. Geniuses have to eat, you know?"

"Yes they do." I laughed because he called me a genius. Tony at best called me a child.

Jade, watch out. You're comparing shit you shouldn't compare.

Whatever. I haven't heard from Tony in a week. This guy is calling me a fucking genius.

Okaaaay.

Ed fed me and then asked me to play over his spins. I was nervous at first, but he was encouraging- not in a shrieking Mrs. Vega way, but in an "I will take you by the hand" way. I was caught up in Ed's kindness. I fell for it... hook, line, and sinker.

Ed put on Robin Thicke's *When I Get You Alone* to spin. He asked me to play the violin lines over it. I had no idea how to do it. Yet, something in his deep black eyes encouraged me to try. His eyes were intense and filled with desire. I raised my bow and played the violin licks over the tracks.

"Excellent!" Ed shouted, eerily sounding like Mrs. Vega. I didn't care about the similarity. I was just proud that I did it. He stopped the music, and I placed my violin down.

"You're very talented. Whoever gets you is a lucky man."

"I hope he thinks so."

"What does that mean?" Ed inquired. His eyes looked intently on mine.

"It means that I don't hear from him as much as I should. He lives in Chicago. I live here," I said. My eyes started to tear up.

"He's foolish. If you were mine, I'd follow you to the end of the earth and then beyond that."

Jade, hunney. Do you smell his game?

Yes, and it's better than being alone.

I blushed, and Ed lifted my hands. I snatched them back as fast as I could. He took my queue and played the Robin Thicke song again for me to rehearse. Ed also played rap songs with violin hooks. I followed suit and got in where I fitted in.

When I played that night, the crowd went wild. I was a star overnight. I felt so confident in my ability that I

200

could have quit school right then and there. But how could I go home to my momma as a college drop out? Ed even paid me half of his earnings. He told me that the show would not have been the same without me.

Ed dropped me off at my dorm. He opened the door and helped me out of the car. His assistance failed me, and I tripped. But he caught me. Although it was a split second, our eyes locked, and he kissed me.

"I'm sorry, but I couldn't help it," he apologized.

"It's okay, but I love someone else. He's my world."

"I know. I hope he treasures you as I would. Please accept my apologies."

"It's okay." I said again.

I hurried away from Ed. I made up my mind that I would not go back to the Blue Flash. I just didn't know how to explain it to Tony. He's going to be so pissed off.

Jade, you fucked up.

I know.

I ran into my room, threw the violin on my desk, and crawled under the covers and cried.

This won't make your problem go away, Jade.

I know.

39

The guilt from Ed's kiss plagued my heart. How could I tell Tony that I kissed someone? I didn't like it. It didn't sit well in my heart, but I had no idea how to make the guilt go away. I didn't want Ed. Ed wanted me. I wanted Tony. Yet, Tony didn't call. If I didn't know any better, I'd say that Tony didn't want me.

But Tony didn't kiss anyone. Did he?

I needed my nagging conscious to stop nagging me. It kept me safe, but since the kiss, it kept me up at night. The kiss gave me nightmares. It made my heart sink.

I stopped eating. I had to tell Tony. I was so scared that he might not love me anymore, but anything is better than the torment my mind was putting me through. So I called him.

"Hello, is Tony there?"

"Yes, Jade?"

"Tony?!" I exclaimed.

Seriously? Out of all the days for him to be home?

Don't chicken out. Tell him.

"Jade, wassup?" He asked me.

"Tony, I have to tell you something."

"Okay. Tell me."

"I was playing a gig Friday night."

"Okay, that's good for you. Congrats. You're playing."

"But that's not it." I stalled.

"What is it?"

203

"I kissed the Deejay."

"You kissed the Deejay?"

"Yes."

Jade, why did you say that? He kissed you!

"-I can't believe you kissed someone. You bitch!"

"What?!"

"I can't do this. I don't want to talk to you. I can't talk to you. "

"Tony, I didn't really kiss him. He kissed me."

"Doesn't matter. Your lips touched someone else's."

"But I didn't want them to."

"Yes, you did. You're such a whore."

"What? I was busting my ass trying to pay for school. I worked three jobs. I'm not getting sleep. I'm not partying. I'm flunking out because I have to work so hard. I only took the gig so that I can get loot because I had to quit two jobs so that I wouldn't flunk out!"

"Doesn't matter. You kissed someone! You touched someone's lips. You're a bitch, and I don't want to be with you anymore."

"First, stop calling me out of my fucking name! Second, you're never there when I call you. You're like that fucking Cake song. What's it called?! '*Never* fucking *there*?!'"

"Well, at least my dick stays in my pants, and I keep my fucking hands to myself!"

"You're a complete asshole!"

"And we're over!" He slammed the phone down. I heard the dial tone. I called him back three times, but he didn't answer. He was there, but he didn't answer. I passed out.

Over the weeks, I called Tony. I sent him snail mail letters, you know, the real kind that the post masters leave at the door. They came back "return to sender". I sent him emails, but they were lost in cyberspace. I fought so hard to keep him, and I lost him over a five second kiss and $200. I lost the love of my life over that shit.

Jade, he wasn't yours to lose.

But I love him.

He wasn't yours. If he was, he'd come back to you.

I wanted to prove myself wrong. I ditched school and hopped on a train to Chicago. I marched right up to Tony's school. I was going to storm the gates. I was going to give it my all and fight for our love. I was going to prove everyone wrong and prove that my love was true and that it was forever.

I emailed Tony. I told him that I was at his campus for a day and that I wanted to see him. He emailed me

206

back saying that he was busy. I was still on academic probation and thus couldn't afford to miss another day of school so I left Chicago and went back. Tony had my heart, but I dropped off my morality in Chicago and picked up some good ole anger. When I got back to school, my fire sign was going to burn everything down. So I did.

It was snowing when I came back to my dorm room. I took everything that belonged to Tony and stuffed it in a bag. I took his shirt that I wore at night. I took his poems, love letters, and jewelry. I was like a furniture clearance sale: Everything must go! And go it did. I scoured my dorm room for anything that reminded me of Tony. I threw everything about him in a plastic bag.

I was so enraged and so far gone that I scared my roommate. I didn't give a fuck about Tony, let alone my roommate. I threw the bag in a corner and left. When I came back, I had a metal garbage can, a lighter, and some lighter fluid.

"What are you doing?" My roommate asked nervously.

"I'm taking the fucking trash out?! Why?"

"Just asking," she said quietly.

Jade, what are you doing?

I'M TAKING OUT THE GODDAMN TRASH. EVERYONE NEEDS TO LEAVE ME THE FUCK ALONE!

I took the bag, the trash can, the matches, and the lighter fluid. I went downstairs and took the garbage out. Something snapped in me as I watched everything burn.

Photos melted into jewelry, which melted into clothes and stuffed animals. Poems turned to black ash. Letters incinerated into their microscopic form. I passionately watched the flames with a brutal triumph destroy all the evidence of Tony's love- our love. I stared as our love combusted into nothingness. By the time I was finished, I had a great, ugly, plastic, ashy, black heap.

Great, it resembles my black heart.

Oh, Jade! Now what do you have?

A giant fucking hole. That's what.

I went upstairs to my room, looked at my roommate, and pretended like nothing happened. I was unraveling at the seams. My new objective was not to be happy, but to feel good.

40

Tony wasn't just mad. He was betrayed. More importantly, he had no love in his heart for me. Around March, I found myself completely alone. If Tony was coming back, he would have come back by Christmas or at least Valentine's Day, but he was a ghost. He was the ghost of my true love's past. Yet, I still couldn't bring myself to say, "Tony who?"

209

I was wasting away and so I dumped all of my energy into playing my violin, doing my school work, and working two jobs instead of one. My grades went up and my playing improved, but my income could not cover my tuition. I was on my way to becoming a street performer after all. It was just a matter of time. I found myself rocking the halls of the Blue Flash to supplement my income. I also found myself becoming adored by more men than just Ed.

I had no time for Ed. As far as I was concerned, he was just a business associate. I lost my lover over his dumb impulse and my fucked up way of communicating. But then again, maybe Tony just wanted to dump me and looked for any reason to do it. I found myself getting enraged again. Thank God I didn't have anything else to burn. I almost got expelled for the last incident. But I didn't fucking care. I was hurting, and it was the only thing I could think of at the time that would give me peace.

Yet, it didn't give me peace. I was still enraged. My fire sign stayed on fire 24/7. I was livid. I just wanted to cool off, in any way that I could. Despite the last snow that fickle March weather sent in, I was still 120 degrees hot. I couldn't take it out on Tony, but I had to take it out on something. My vagina was a viable option, and I just needed to get laid. So I did.

If there was one thing I knew about musicians, it was that they all had groupies. It didn't make a difference if one was a male musician or female musician either. I had a ton, too. Men would always want to buy me drinks after a set or two. I always turned them down because I liked to walk home sober and also because I was underage. After that last incident, I didn't trust getting into cars with guys, and a clear head was necessary for a single lady's survival, especially while walking alone on a college campus late at night. But something was different in me that night. I was on the prowl.

Other than Tony, I couldn't find any other attractive souls. Tony had everything I wanted in a man. He was the perfect height. He had the perfect eyes and hair. Most importantly, he had the perfect swag and mind. Tony wasn't afraid to challenge me. He wasn't afraid of a lot of things. I found that to be irresistible.

My momma always said that pretty girls don't stay single forever and that I was no different. My momma also told me that pretty, talented, and smart girls were a triple threat. Plus, she raised me to be independent, which she believed was a bonus. Hence, I wouldn't stay on the shelves long. But I still didn't want anybody else but Tony.

Jade, you gotta get over this dude. This is the second time he's broken your heart. He's not worth it.

I know.

212

Do you?

Look, I don't have to prove shit to you. I can get any guy I want in this bitch!

How about him?

My conscience was pointing to a tall, slender guy with blonde hair. He was Tonyesque, but not quite right. Yet, he was cute and possibly my next objective or distraction.

Although I was cute, I had not been sexy for anyone in a long time. Yet, that didn't stop me. My momma always said, "Once you got it, you got it!" Later, I learned that was true about a lot of things in life, including sex and riding bikes.

I gathered up what little confidence I had and multiplied it times ten. Being a Leo made it especially easy to get my mojo going. I walked right up to him and asked him his name. He told me that his name was Brian. I told

213

him my name and asked if I could have his phone number. He searched for a pen and paper. He found a black sharpie, but he could not find any paper.

I pealed back his shirt and wrote my phone number on his lower abdomen. I told him to call me if he could ever find the time to come out and play. He called me around three am that same evening. I got in cab around four am, and I blew his mind until school started around nine am. Yup, I still had it.

I loved Brian and our "study" sessions. He was an art major with a minor in photography and loved taking my pictures. I loved being the center of attention- his attention. I was the subject of most of his work- mostly, his nude work. He would listen to my new songs. We offered feedback to each other. Then we'd play in the bed, in the kitchen, and on the floor for the next six hours.

As always, all good things come to an end. It was like that with Tony. I expected it with Brian. So when he left me for his ex-girlfriend, I wasn't too upset. I just accepted it and moved on. I still thought it was pretty fucking bogus that this chick could get her ex-boyfriend back with a wink and a smile, but, meanwhile, my heart was smeared all over Tony's fucking shoes. Go fucking figure.

But when things ended with Brian, I had that good ole bounce back. I was like: "Next!" There were no shortages of guys on campus. This guppy was turning into a full blown shark!

41

By April, the sting of Tony's absence lay heavy on my heart, but I grew tired of the quick fix: fucking. The same skit played over and over. It was getting boring. I was getting over it.

Random guy number whatever: "Wassup?"

Me: "Us."

Then we'd fuck. Some men were tasty. Some weren't so tasty. But they would all meet their inevitable fate: a sudden departure from my life. They were just too vanilla- not as in white, but as in bland. Same height. Same size. Same bullshit. So I stuck to studying, practicing my violin, and working my ass off, and it paid off too.

By the time final grades came out in May, I found myself in central Illinois' tornado season holding two letters in my hand. I was running late for work when I found them in my mailbox and so I stuffed them in my backpack. They weren't my usual credit card bills. They were official letters from the university. I needed to know what they were. I rushed to open them as I headed to my bus stop.

I opened the letter from my department first. It read: "Congratulations, Jade Valentine. We proudly inform you that you've made the Dean's List. Take pride in this momentous occasion. Signed, The College of Liberal Arts and Sciences."

My face beamed with pride. I was in such a great mood and rushed to open the next letter. It read: "Dear Jade Valentine: We regret to inform you that you have not paid your tuition in full. As a result, we have dropped you from enrollment for the next semester. Your transcripts will also be on hold until we receive your payment in full. Signed, The Registrar's Office."

As if the Greek Gods read my heart, the sky opened up and sheets of rain poured down. I wasn't Wiley Coyote or some other Loony Toon with a black rain cloud over my head. I was grateful for the pouring rain. It hid the tears running down my cheeks. It concealed my failure.

I felt total and utter despair. It seemed like every time I tried to excel at something, something pulled me back ten steps. I wanted to fling my body off the nearest campus building. But I quickly dismissed it.

Jade, you know, nothing worth achieving is easy to come by.

True, but why is everything so fucking hard for me?

I don't know, babe. I don't know.

All I could do was go to work, especially since I gave up my dick-hunting hobby. I needed to get my mind off of my failure. According to my university, I was now a homeless and expelled college student, but at least I had a job. No, I had two fucking jobs and no money. And I can't pay for school? What the fuck?

42

I couldn't go back to Chicago as a failure. I couldn't look my mom and dad in the eye and tell them that I

218

couldn't do what they sent me away to college to do: succeed. I found another job waiting tables at a shitty local diner. The tips were good and helped me make rent.

Unfortunately, I was now a townie- a permanent fixture in the town that I was supposed to leave with a degree. I rented a room in an apartment with three girls who knew each other from childhood. They were very pretty and rich but had nothing going on upstairs... and I mean nothing. They had no aspirations and no ambitions other than finding a rich guy to marry, have babies, and combine trust funds.

I laughed at the thought that life was easier for them. They were skinny, beautiful, Barbie-like, and filthy rich. I would watch men damn near break their necks to open doors and their wallets for them. They had no pride. They didn't need to have pride. They reminded me of old

219

films in which the lady in frilly lingerie stated that you can never be too rich or too skinny. They all had both.

I thought that maybe God thought that people like them needed more help and so he gave them more of everything. I thought that maybe people who struggled and hustled were more mentally equipped and thus could handle a harder life. I finally figured out what Billy Holiday's *God Bless the Child* meant. It meant that God favored struggle people. Right?

Ha! Jade, that's what "struggle people" tell themselves to make them feel better- to make life feel easier. You know, that's bullshit, right?

Yup. But I need to feel better. I am struggle people.

Touché, Jade. Touché.

I was struggling, too. My parents knew that I wasn't in school. They also knew that I was struggling. They begged me to come back home, but I would not come back home defeated. I lost so much to make it to that school. I lost Tony. No! I would stay in my struggle and hustle my way out without anyone's help.

I didn't need a prince. I didn't need a fairy godmother or a benefactor. As long as I had my drive, I could save myself. As long as I was alive, I would fight. However, a benefactor would waltz into my life whether I wanted him to or not.

His name was Raj. He walked into my restaurant and the hostess sat him in my section. I saw him immediately. He had jet black hair and warm brown eyes. He also had strong muscular arms emerging under his blue scrubs. He was the most beautiful man I had seen in my life- well, second to Tony.

I made my way over to his table. He asked me for a cup of coffee: "black". He smiled at me when he ordered it that way. I knew he was flirting, but I was covered in biscuits, gravy, and whatever else I served that day. Surely

he couldn't be flirting with me. But he was.

"What's your name?" he asked.

"Jade." I said bluntly. I didn't want no parts of him.

He looked untouchable, and I had it up to my till in men.

My vagina needed a rest as well.

"Jade? Jade? That name sounds familiar. You don't

hang out at the Blue Flash, do you?"

"Yes. No." I stammered.

"Well, do you?" He snapped.

"No and yes. You see, I play the violin over the

deejay's spins sometimes. I work there, so I don't really

hang out there."

"That's right! I knew that you looked familiar. I've

watched you play. You're simply amazing. Why are you

working here?" He asked impatiently, with a tinge of

disappointment.

"Thank you. And it's a really long, complicated story- a story that I don't feel like getting into."

"I like long stories. Have dinner with me tonight. It won't be here." He assured me.

"Thank you, but no thank you," I said firmly.

"Did I forget to mention that I am a doctor?"

I overturned his mug and poured him a cup of coffee- black.

"That's great for you, but still no. I'm sorry. If you don't want anything else, here's your check," I said firmly as I whipped out his check in lightning speed.

"Look, I am going to sit in your section every day until you go out with me," he protested defiantly.

"Okay, we can go eat, but I work a lot, and I don't have time in my schedule."

This guy won't quit. Will he, Jade?

Nope.

223

"Hey, you can wear your work clothes, and I will take you anywhere you need to go. Did I mention I have a Jaguar?"

"Again, great for you. Us working folk have to ride the bus," I said, as sarcastically as I could muster at a customer.

"Did I mention that you're beautiful?"

"Did you mention that you're annoying?" I asked. He chuckled.

Jade, is this guy for real? He acts like you're on the menu.

Yup. Well, he can't fucking have me.

"So whaduya say? Dinner? Me?"

"Whaduya say?" Jade fucking run!

I know right! Wassup with that fucking line?

"One dinner," I conceded in defeat. "Then, please get the hell out of my section!" I rolled my eyes, took my coffee pot, and walked away.

"Yes, ma'am!" He shouted at the top of his lungs.

Great... the whole fucking diner knows.

"Wait, what's your name?" I asked. He was so caught up in knowing my name that he forgot to give me his.

"Raj."

"Raj?"

"Yes, it means Kingdom. I'm Indian. Not American Indian, but Indian Indian." He laughed. I smiled. It was the first smile I wore since I was with Tony- since I was in his arms.

Raj took me to an Italian restaurant that same night. We drank wine even though I was underage. The people knew him there and waited on him hand and foot.

He treated me like a queen. He listened intently as I told him my story.

I told him about my family, my goals, and my dreams. He listened intently as I talked to him about working three jobs and being kicked out of school. He looked at me with kindness. His eyes didn't judge me. He genuinely cared about my life. He was warm. He was a gentleman.

Raj dropped me off at my apartment and left. The hospital paged him and he had to leave urgently. He told me that he would call me tomorrow. He did. I enjoyed Raj's company. He was funny and sweet. Moreover, he was completely addicted to me.

He saw me every day that he didn't have to work. Sometimes, he would get off of a long shift and pick me up when I had free time-although I didn't have much free time anyway. When I wasn't with Raj, I was working. Girl's gotta eat and have someplace to sleep. Yet, between all of our shifts, I was happy with Raj.

More importantly, I was happy paying my own way. I was proud that I didn't need a man to take care of me. I was an independent woman! I was struggling, but I was happy. I had my pride to keep me warm! But Raj wanted to be the only one keeping me warm. He took me out to the place where we had our first date and asked me the big question.

"Jade?"

"Yes?"

"Look, I really like you. I love being with you. Why don't you move in with me?"

"Huh?" I was puzzled and scared. "Raj, I can't move in with you. I am under a lease."

"Break it. I'll pay it. Just live with me."

"Um, I don't know. This is just too fast. I need to think about it."

"Look, it makes the most sense. You can live with me and that way you won't have to pay living expenses. You can pay off your school's 'back tuition' in no time."

"True, but it's a big step."

"I want to be with you. You want to be with me, right?"

No.

"Yes." I lied. Raj was so sweet. I couldn't break his heart. I knew how that felt, and I didn't want anyone else to feel that way.

"Plus, I can hear you play every day."

"True."

"Great. It's settled. I'll pick you up from your house tomorrow. We will break your lease and that will be that!"

"Okay." I stammered.

The next day, Raj was true to his word. He picked me up. He moved me out and paid for my lease. I broke my lease that day and left my independence it on a shelf in my old apartment. I left it in exchange for the hope of getting back to school and for a new life with Raj.

43

Before I moved in with my Raj, I called my momma and asked her if I should move out of my apartment to live with Raj. To my surprise, she answered in the affirmative.

"Darling, doctors don't grow on trees. Doctors, who worship the ground you walk on, don't fall from the sky neither. Didn't I teach you anything?"

"But momma, what about love? I don't think I love him."

"Love is overrated. Love breaks your heart, and love doesn't pay the bills. Doctors, on the other hand, do."

229

As much as I hated to say it, my momma was right. Doctors do pay the bills, and Raj paid for everything. Whatever I wanted, he got it for me. If I looked at something, it was wrapped up before I could even say that I wanted it. It was nice of him, and I was extremely grateful not living on ramen and candy bars. Yet, deep down inside, I hated it. I think I even hated him for it.

The castle he moved me into felt more like an elaborate prison than a home. The leather sofas and the tapestries were my guards making sure I didn't move-literally. The vaulted ceilings laughed at my dreams. The sconces and granite countertops checked my pride. The cashmere rugs pointed rifles at me, daring me to escape.

If Raj's house was my prison, Raj was my warden. His eyes went from warm and endearing to judgmental and cold. I couldn't grasp the red flags at first. I was blinded by the bling and his promises of marriage.

Raj was the first man ever who asked me to marry him. I was scared of the possibility of being his wife, but I was happy that someone chose me. It meant that I was wife material. I wasn't just someone's exotic conquest or somebody's play thing. I was more than just a good time.

Yet, the pride of being a doctor's wife was trumped by my fear of being a wife. I didn't want to throw away my dreams of being a great performer or getting my degree. But Raj had a different idea of what a wife meant. It meant throwing my dreams away. At first, I wouldn't let him, but then I did. I felt that I owed him, and that meant fulfilling his absurd requests.

First, Raj wanted me to quit all of my jobs. He told me that he would pay off my tuition and that I would be in school within the next semester. Like a fool, I quit all three jobs. When I would ask him if he sent the check, he told me that it was on its way. The check was always on its way, but it never got there- ever!

Second, I found myself with nothing to do. After I quit my jobs, I did nothing but play my violin, clean his home, cook his food, and ride his cock. I was lonely and sad. I found myself eagerly waiting for Raj to come home from work- not because I liked him or loved him, but because I desperately needed someone to talk to. Yet, Raj didn't want to talk when he got home. Raj wanted to eat and fuck in his clean house. This was my new life. I wanted my old one back, struggle and all.

44

I made up my mind to leave Raj. I had no choice. I was wasting my life in his prison. I was not going to be another "should have could have would have". I was going to take whatever strength I had and leave. But I needed help. I called my momma.

232

"Momma, I want to leave. Can I come back home?"

"Baby, what's wrong?"

"It's Raj. Something isn't right. He wants me to cook, clean, and throw my dreams away."

"Is that it?"

"What do you mean 'is that it'?"

"Baby, you're a woman."

"So?"

"So women must make sacrifices."

"Well, I'm a person first. Why should I sacrifice my dreams, only to be with someone that I really didn't want to be with in the first damn place?"

"Baby, what's the alternative?"

"My freedom is the goddamn alternative!" I slammed the phone down on my mother. She called me back twice. But I didn't answer. Fuck sacrifices. If I wasn't

233

sure of it, I was going to leave Raj today. He wasn't going to bring me down. Not over my dead body!

I waited for Raj to come home. I had my bags packed. I was going back to Chicago. Living with Raj was not a viable option. I bought my ticket, scheduled my cab, and waited for Raj. A smarter me would have left him a fucking note, but I wasn't the type to run from confrontation. I wasn't going to start running then. Looking back, I should have ran.

"Hi Raj. How was your day?"

"Um good. You going on a trip, baby? I know you wanted to see your family. How long are you staying?"

"Until I can find a new apartment, Raj."

"Huh?"

"I can't do this anymore. I'm sorry. I don't want you to hate me, but I can't live like this."

"Like what? Like a pampered bitch?"

"Excuse the hell out of me? I am no one's bitch."

"No. You're my bitch, and you're not going anywhere!"

"I'm sorry, but you must have lost your fucking mind. I do what the fuck I want! And I don't want you."

"No. It's me who wants you. You don't think I know that you don't love me? You moved in here. I paid for your clothes. I paid for your food. I put a roof over your head. You need me! You owe me!"

"Um, reality check. I had a job before I met you. I actually had three."

"Yes, and now look where you live… in a fucking castle. I swear you're such an ungrateful slut."

"That's the last time that you're going to call me out of my name, Raj."

"Well, what are you going to do?"

"I don't have to do shit but leave. Thank you, but no thank you!" I said as firmly as I could muster.

I picked up my purse and my suitcases. I didn't have any belongings other than what was packed. Raj said my apartment stuff was "college tacky" and threw them away. I was glad he did because it made my move so much easier in the end. I reached for the door handle and fell to the floor.

When I came to, Raj had his hands tightly clasping my throat. I couldn't breathe. I thought I was going to die. I wanted to die. I wanted to stop fighting. I didn't even know what I was fighting for. I gave in, but something snapped inside me.

Jade, fucking fight! You can't fight this whole time and then throw in the fucking towel now! What the fuck is wrong with you?!

Fuck. Okay. Fuck!!!

236

I picked up the golden Hindu statue that lay by the door and cracked Raj's skull. He fell down instantly. I grabbed my purse and my suitcases and ran the hell out. But before I left, I paused and watched the blood leak from Raj's brain and circle the statue. Thank you, Ganesha, Hindu God of removing barriers. The irony made me laugh frantically.

I called 911 from a neighbor's house. I told the cops what happened and that they should send an ambulance. I told the cops that I could be reached at my friend's house and not to look for me at my neighbor's home. The cops told me not to leave the town.

I left town anyway. I knew Raj wouldn't press charges. His pride wouldn't let him state on any public record that the all-mighty doctor was brought down by a simple waitress. Fuck Raj. I do what I want. I made up my mind that day that no man would ever put me on a pedestal or glass shelf again. Ever!

45

I moved back to Chicago that November. I told my momma what happened. She was nicer than I thought that she would be. I thought she would make me go back to Raj. I thought that she would say that being choked was one of the sacrifices that a woman had to make, but she didn't.

My momma was extremely livid and extremely apologetic. She told me that there were some sacrifices a woman should never make. On the top of that list was safety.

"If a man puts his hand on you, he doesn't love you. Move on."

"Yes, momma."

"I didn't raise you to be nobody's punching bag."

"Yes, momma."

I took comfort in my momma's words. They were like a warm blanket on a cold day, and I especially needed it. This November was extremely cold for Chicago, but my body was on fire. I thought that it was from anger, regret, or sadness. It was actually from pregnancy. Raj was going to stay in my life no matter what, but I wouldn't let him. Never again.

I wasn't scared as much as I was nervous. I knew what my momma would say before she'd say it. She'd say a baby is a gift from God. She would beg me not to get rid of her grandchild. NO. I couldn't tell my mother that I was pregnant, but I needed advice. I couldn't bring myself to call my dad either. So I called Tony.

I picked up the phone, and dialed Tony's cell. My hands were shaking profusely. He answered.

Thank God he answered.

"Tony?"

"Jade?"

"Yes. Tony. I need some advice. I don't know what to do. Do you have time?"

"Yes. What's going on? You sound really upset."

"I'm pregnant. I can't tell the guy because of an incident. I am really thinking about getting an abortion."

"What?! You're pregnant?! What the fuck is wrong with you?"

"Nothing is wrong with me!"

"You know, I always thought you were special. I always thought that you had great potential. I never thought I would see you throw everything away."

"What?" My head was swimming, and my heart was aching. The love of my life was basically calling me a complete fuck up. I couldn't take it, especially after everything I just went through. I mustered the only words I could think of: "Fuck you!"

I hung up the phone. Fuck Tony.

I called my stepmother and told her everything. I was determined to get an abortion. I didn't want to be tied to Raj for the rest of my life. I didn't want to be tied to anything!

My stepmother gathered the money from my dad. She simply told him that the money was for me. She didn't give him any specifics. Looking back, I think my dad knew what the money was for. He was just simply speechless.

46

My stepmother accompanied me to a local abortion clinic. I sat nervously in the hard chairs with twenty other girls in similar circumstances. I watched them all as they walked into the back rooms and then back out a couple hours later. I waited for hours and watched some girls leave without having the procedure done at all.

My mind was pacing back and forth in my skull. I knew I couldn't have Raj's baby. He was controlling and abusive. More importantly, I didn't love him. I could never have someone's seed in me if it didn't come from love, and it didn't come from love. It came from Raj, and I still loved Tony.

My stepmother looked lovingly at me. I was glad that she came with me because I might have run out of the room. She held my hand. I wished she was holding me. I knew that at any moment it would be my turn, and she would have to let go of my hand. I wanted to cry, but my tear ducts were dry.

"Jade? Jade?" A short nurse in lavender scrubs summoned me.

"Yes?" I stood up.

242

"Follow me."

"Yes, ma'am."

She took me into a small, dull grey room. It was cold. She asked for my contact information and payment. After she went over the risks of the procedure, the anesthesia, and every other risky outcome that some lawyer imagined, she asked me if I was sure that I wanted to go through with it.

"Yes. I'm sure," I said.

"Good. We'll take an ultrasound to make sure that you're pregnant."

"Do you want to see the picture?"

"No, what kind of question is that?" I snapped.

"Relax. It's just so we can see if you're really pregnant."

"Why would I be here if I was not pregnant?"

"You'd be surprised how many girls come here and aren't pregnant."

"Okay."

The nurse took me into another room that was slightly larger. I lay on the hospital bed and the ultrasound tech came in. The jelly was cold on my belly and then got warm as she moved the wand all over my lower abdomen.

"Do you want to hear the heart beat?" the ultrasound tech asked.

"No! I wish people stop asking me about me seeing and hearing things," I snapped.

"My apologies. You're pregnant. We'll prep you for surgery. You have an anesthesiologist, so you will need to get completely undressed."

"Okay. Whatever," I muttered.

The lavender nurse came back in the room and ushered me to a locker room.

"You're one of the last two women for today, so take your time."

"Thank you."

I got undressed and threw on my hospital gown. The lavender nurse came back with a chart and ushered me to a new hospital bed. I climbed on it and noticed that there were several people in the room. They were wearing masks and surgical gear. One of the masked men came up to me.

"Hi. I'm your anesthesiologist. We're going to place this mask on your face before the procedure. I want you to count back from 100 to 1, okay?"

"Okay."

He placed the mask on my face.

"100...99...98..."

47

Nurse Claire pushed Jade into the recovery room. She looked at her bronze skin as her arm fell from under the hospital covers.

"Poor baby. This one looks really young, too," Nurse Claire said.

Just then Jade started moving and screaming.

"What, honey? Hey, Dr. Stanley can you please come here?"

Dr. Stanley walked in and noticed Nurse Claire's frantic face.

"What is it?" he said.

"She won't stop screaming."

"She's just having a nightmare. Just watch her."

"Tony... Tony... Tony!" Jade screamed.

"She's calling for someone named, Tony," said Nurse Claire.

"Hmmm, see if he's out in the waiting room."

"Okay," Nurse Claire obliged. "No one's out there, just some woman," shouted Nurse Claire.

"Just find him," Dr. Stanley demanded.

"Excuse me, ma'am... Is someone named Tony with you?"

"No," stated Jade's stepmom. "I'm here waiting for my daughter."

"Okay, thank you."

Nurse Claire walked into the recovery room and held Jade's hand. "Poor baby. Poor, poor baby."

48

I came to and quickly put on my clothes. I grabbed my antibiotics and jetted out of the door. I was more determined than ever to get my life together. My stepmother looked worried.

"How did it go?" she asked.

247

"I don't know. I don't remember it. Last thing I said was 99."

"Okay," she said. "You know, Jade, the nurse was looking for someone named Tony."

"Oh really? What a coincidence! I hope her Tony is better than mine," I laughed.

49

December in Chicago was always cold and dreary. It was even colder and drearier when you were without a job or a pot to piss in and a window to throw it out. I put in applications all over the city. Doors were closed, and no one was hiring. I couldn't work, which meant that I couldn't pay my back tuition. I couldn't even fucking think.

I knew one thing for sure. It was time that I started asking others for assistance. It was time that I checked my pride. It was time that I got the fuck out of Chicago.

Not only could I not find a job, but every inch of the city reminded me of my love. It reminded me of Tony. It reminded me of failure. I was failing fast. I hated failing. I called my dad.

I found myself at my daddy's mercy. To my surprise, he wanted to help. He listened and did not give me some obscure solution to solve my real problems. I was stunned. He was actually helpful.

"What do you want?"

"I want to go."

"Go where?"

"I want to go to Europe and become a street performer. Then I want to play in their symphony halls. I want to play in a real orchestra that plays for real operas. I want to go. I need to go. I'm dying if I stay here."

"Okay," my dad gave in.

"Okay?"

249

"Yes. Okay! Go baby, and I will give you some money to get you started."

"You're not mad at me? You're not disappointed with me for not finishing school?"

"What? Get out of here. Fuck school. Music is in your veins. You only got one life to live, so live it by your own standards. Don't live it by anyone else's. And never let anyone take your music from you."

Great, Jade. Now he fucking tells you?

Well, at least he's telling me.

A couple of months later, my daddy bought me a one way ticket to Paris and stuffed a thousand dollars into my pocket. He drove me to the airport. We both got out of the car.

"You got your passport?" He asked.

"Yes, daddy."

"I'm so proud of you. You make me so happy."

250

"Thanks, daddy!"

My dad gave me a bear hug and left. I was off on my own, following my dreams. I took out my cell phone and called Tony one last time.

"Tony?"

"Yes. Jade?"

"Yes. Tony. It's me. I'm leaving for Europe."

"Europe?"

"Yes. I am. I don't know when I am coming back so I just wanted to say goodbye."

"Why Europe?"

"Because I am going to play, even if I die trying."

"Okay. Well, good luck," he said dryly.

"Is there anything else you want to say?" I pleaded.

"Nope. Just stay safe. Don't get kidnapped. Goodbye."

"Goodbye."

One tear fell down my face courtesy of Tony fucking Georgino. The January Chicago wind dried it up as if it never existed. I gathered my strength to leave everything behind. I dumped my cell phone in the trash can. I wouldn't need it anyway. I walked to the check-in line and passed my reflection on a chrome pillar. I looked very distorted, but I also looked very strong. I got my plane ticket, checked my bags and my violin, and left the U.S. and everything I knew behind... because fuck that.

50

I got to Paris ten hours later and one day earlier, I think. I found a room and a job. It's funny that I had to leave the country before I had an opportunity to work a meaningful job. I found a permanent gig playing my violin at a local café. It was in the American tourist district and so I really didn't have to learn French.

I played my violin for the Café de Americana and in exchange, I got room and board. I also got notoriety. People would come in and sit with their lovers or other family members, and I would play classical violin with a jazz twist. Sometimes, I got to sing.

I especially loved the Paris nights. I had a bigger crowd and more opportunities to be heard. I was living in Paris for six months when the conductor of the La Philharmonie came into my café. He waited until I was done with my set.

He walked up to me, gave me his card, uttered only two words, and left.

His two words: "show up". So I did.

I showed up. I auditioned for a spot in the orchestra, got the gig, and worked my ass off.

I worked so hard that I even earned a spot for second chair. A year later, I was first chair. Two years later, my name was on the marquee. I wasn't playing on spinning records in a dismal bar in Small town, Illinois. I was playing in Paris, Italy, and London. I became Jade Valentine: Violinist Extraordinaire! I could even hear Mrs. Vega screaming, "Excellence!"

My violin was a big part of my life, but it wasn't the only part. I met a guy named Franco. We got married after knowing each other for only two months. We had passion. We had intensity. We got divorced one month later.

Two years later, when I toured Italy, I met Jacque. I thought it was weird that I married an Italian guy in Paris and a French guy in Italy. But the one thing I knew about my life was that it was everything but normal. I gave Jacque three beautiful kids, but we couldn't last. I left Jacque after ten years of marriage, a mortgage, and a dog.

Even with the house, the kids, the husband, and the career, something was missing. I didn't know what it was until I got a voice message.

"Hey Jade. It's Tony. I'll be in Paris soon. I'd like to see you. Call me back."

I checked the voice mail three times to get Tony's whole number. It was fifteen years later, but my heart felt like it was a day ago. I had no idea what Tony wanted, but I was going to find out.

51

I was going to see Tony. As a matter of fact, I was determined to see Tony. I was determined to tell him what I thought, and he had no choice but to listen. There was no phone that he could hang up on me while pulling my heart from my chest in some *Mortal Kombat* fashion. NO! He would have to look upon me, face-to-face, and take it. He was going to man up and "learn today!"

255

I was going to tell him what I thought of him. I was going to tell him how he hurt me. I was going to give him the business. He wanted to see me? Well, he would have to hear an ear load first.

I was too excited to tell him off. He walked into the room, and I lost all my words. He looked like I remembered. He was cute. He was dorky. He was...

Jade!!!!

He was mine!

I forgot how much I hated him. I forgot how much he hurt me. I forgot how to speak. He picked up on my queue and spoke first.

Thank God he's smart.

"Hey, Jade. You look great."

"Thanks. You look awesome yourself."

"Well, it's not hard when you're as fly as me," he smirked. I laughed.

"Don't you mean as smug and as dorky as you are?" I bantered back. Oh I loved our banter even now.

"Anyways, I wanted to see you. Jade. Plus, we're here, and my wife wanted to go to your show."

"Wife?"

"Yes. I have a wife."

"Oh, good for you."

"So do you think you can get us in?"

"Hmmm."

I paused. I thought maybe he can hear my heart explode.

You know, he can't hear that, Jade?

You're right, but he can hear something else!

Just then, all of the rage that I had forgotten over the last fifteen years and ten seconds welled up inside the back of my throat. I was an eternal flame. I was enraged. I was fucking angry! Before I knew it, I was yelling.

257

"Sit down. How dare you come to my place of business and ask me for fucking tickets?"

"Now, Jade…"

"No, shut up you fucking douche. You dumped me over a fucking phone conversation fifteen years ago. You knew I loved you. You knew I needed you. You knew I wanted to have your kids and be married to your trifling ass. You knew I gave you my heart. You'd always tell me that you were not the marrying type or that we were too young to love. Now you show up fucking married?"

"Jade, we were young. We didn't know what love was."

"Speak for your Goddamn self! I knew what I wanted. I always knew what I wanted. You were what I always wanted. And you wanted me too, but you discarded me like I was nothing. You discarded me as if you didn't lie awake thinking about me. You discarded me as if you could exist without me. You discarded me like you didn't inhale me, like you didn't breathe me! You stole my soul mate from me, and you tell me that you're married? Fuck you!"

"I don't know what you want from me, Jade. I don't know what you want me to say."

"I want you to acknowledge us. I want to know that I was not some conquest or some flavor of the fucking month. I want to know that you loved me as much as I loved you. I want to know that you fought for us as much as I did. I want to know that there is a hole in your heart like the one I still have. I want you to tell me the goddamn truth!"

"That would solve nothing! I'm still married. I can't give you what you want, Jade. I could never really give you what you want. I'm so sorry."

"Well, Tony. That's the most honest thing that you have ever told me. Goodbye... and take these fucking tickets with you. I hope your wife loves my fucking show!"

"We won't be going!"

"No, I want you to go and enjoy yourselves. I really do. I just needed to get that off my chest. Fifteen years is a lot of time to possess pent up rage over a spineless asshole who broke your heart over a goddamn telephone call," I said, relaxed with a new calm over my face.

"Pent up rage?" Tony saw my face relax and began to relax as well.

"Yes. You broke my heart not once. Today makes the fifth fucking time! You will not break my heart anymore. I'm taking my fucking power back."

"You mad at me?"

"No. I'm not. Well, I was when I said all of that, but not anymore!"

"Why not? What changed in these last few seconds?"

"One: I got that off my chest. Two: I love you. I will always love you. I will always want to have your babies. I will always want to be your wife. That will never change."

"So why are you giving me and my wife these tickets?"

"Because Tony, I do what the fuck I want!"

Tony left my greenroom with his tickets and watched me as I rocked the fucking house.

La Fin (French for I'm fucking done!)

Afterword:

I like to thank everyone who helped me in producing this novel. I would like to dedicate this novel to them. I would also like to dedicate this novel to my sons, so they have an idea on how crazy a woman can get when she really loves a man. Boys, if you find a girl like Jade, you should keep her. I would also like to dedicate this novel to Renada, my UK friend, so that you may have something spicy to read at your book club meetings.

Moreover, I would like to dedicate this novel to any and every girl or woman who has loved someone beyond themselves. I think love keeps us human. Yet, to experience true love is divine and remarkable.

Last, I would like to dedicate this novel to anyone who has experienced true love, lost it, and now has given up on finding love again. -For those, I want you to forget

No Fairy Tales

the concept of loving the one you're with if you can't be with the one you love. People make mistakes, but the problem is that we don't go back and fix our mistakes. We move on- most often to the wrong person because we are not honest with ourselves on what we truly want and who we truly love.

So if you truly love an individual with all of your heart, don't move on right away. Go back and fight or at least try to fight for them within reason….WITHIN REASON without breaching the peace. If that person is firm in their "no" and are placing a restraining order on you, then please move on.

BUT if such person is willing to give you a shot, then go for it because you only have one life to live. You might as well spend it with your soul mate especially if they are still living. Quit wasting your precious time.

Made in the USA
Lexington, KY
03 April 2015